THE F… BOOK OF HORROR

Edited by Kurt Singer

TARGET

A TARGET BOOK

published by
the Paperback Division of
W. H. Allen & Co. PLC

A Target Book
Published in 1985
by the Paperback Division of
W. H. Allen & Co. PLC
44 Hill Street, London W1X 8LB

These stories were first selected by Kurt Singer for inclusion in his anthology *Tales From the Unknown* (W. H. Allen 1970).

Printed in Great Britain by
Hunt Barnard Printing Ltd., Aylesbury, Bucks.

ISBN 0 426 201876

CONTENTS

The Haunted and the Haunters
or, The House and the Brain

Lord Lytton

A friend of mine, who is a man of letters and a philosopher, said to me one day, as if between jest and earnest: 'Fancy! since we last met, I have discovered a haunted house in the midst of London.'

'Really haunted? – and by what? – ghosts?'

'Well, I can't answer that question; all I know is this: six weeks ago my wife and I were in search of a furnished apartment. Passing a quiet street, we saw on the window of one of the houses a bill, "Apartments, Furnished". The situation suited us: we entered the house – liked the rooms – engaged them by the week – and left them the third day. No power on earth could have reconciled my wife to stay longer; and I don't wonder at it.'

'What did you see?'

'Excuse me – I have no desire to be ridiculed as a superstitious dreamer – nor, on the other hand, could I ask you to accept on my affirmation what you would hold to be incredible without the evidence of your own senses. Let me say only this, it was not so much what we saw or heard (in which you might fairly suppose that we were the dupes of our own excited fancy, or the victims of the imposture in others) that drove us away, as it was an undefinable terror which seized both of us whenever we passed by the door of a certain unfurnished room, in which we neither saw nor heard anything. And the strangest marvel of all was, that for once in my life I agreed with my wife, silly woman though she be – and allowed, after the third night, that it was impossible to stay a fourth in that house. Accordingly, on the fourth morning I summoned the woman who kept the house and attended on us, and told her that the rooms did not quite suit us, and we would not stay out our week. She said dryly: "I know why; you have stayed longer than any other lodger. Few ever stayed a second night; none before you a third. But I take it they have been very kind to you."

'"They – who?" I asked, affecting to smile.

'"Why, they who haunt the house, whoever they are. I don't mind them; I remember them many years ago, when I lived in this house, not as a servant; but I know they will be the death of me some day. I don't care – I'm old, and must die soon anyhow; and then I shall be with them, and in this house still." The woman spoke with so dreamy a calmness, that really it was a sort of awe that prevented my conversing with her further. I paid for my week, and too happy were my wife and I to get off so cheaply.'

'You excite my curiosity,' said I; 'nothing I should like better than to a sleep in a haunted house. Pray give me the address of the one which you left so ignominiously.'

My friend gave me the address; and when we parted, I walked straight towards the house thus indicated.

It is situated on the north side of Oxford Street, in a dull but respectable thoroughfare. I found the house shut up – no bill at the window, and no response to my knock. As I was turning away, a beer-boy, collecting pewter pots at the neighbouring areas, said to me: 'Do you want anyone at that house, sir?'

'Yes, I heard it was to be let.'

'Let! – why, the woman who kept it is dead – has been dead these three weeks, and no one can be found to stay there, though Mr J – offered ever so much. He offered mother, who chars for him, a pound a week just to open and shut the windows, and she would not.'

'Would not! – and why?'

'The house is haunted; and the old woman who kept it was found dead in her bed, with her eyes wide open. They say the devil strangled her.'

'Pooh! – you speak of Mr J – . Is he the owner of the house?'

'Yes.'

'Where does he live?'

'In G – Street, number – .'

'What is he? – in any business?'

'No, sir – nothing particular; a single gentleman.'

I gave the pot-boy the gratuity earned by his liberal information, and proceeded to Mr J – , in G – Street, which was close by the street that boasted the haunted house. I was lucky enough to find Mr J – at home – an elderly man, with intelligent countenance and prepossessing manners.

I communicated my name and my business frankly. I said I heard the house was considered to be haunted – that I had a strong desire to examine the house with so equivocal a reputation – that I should be greatly obliged if he would allow me to hire it, though only for a night. I was willing to pay for that privilege whatever he might be inclined to ask. 'Sir,' said Mr J – , with great courtesy, 'the house is at your service, for as short or as long a time as you please. Rent is out of the question – the obligation will be on my side should you be able to discover the cause of the strange phenomena which at present deprive it of all value. I cannot let it, for I cannot even get a servant to keep it in order or answer the door. Unluckily the house is haunted, if I may use that expression, not only by night, but by day; though at night the disturbances are of a more unpleasant and sometimes of a more alarming character. The poor old woman who died in it three weeks ago was a pauper whom I took out of the workhouse, for in her childhood she had been known to some of my family, and had once been in such good circumstances that she had rented that house of my uncle. She was a woman of superior education and strong mind, and was the only person I could ever induce to remain in the house. Indeed, since her death, which was sudden, and the coroner's inquest, which gave it a notoriety in the neighbourhood, I have so despaired of finding any person to take charge of the house, much more a tenant, that I would willingly let it rent free for a year to anyone who would pay its rates and taxes.'

'How long is it since the house acquired this sinister character?'

'That I can scarcely tell you, but very many years since. The old woman I spoke of said it was haunted when she rented it between thirty and forty years ago. The fact is, that my life has been spent in the East Indies, and in the civil service of the Company. I returned to England last year, on inheriting the fortune of an uncle, among whose possessions was the house in question. I found it shut up and uninhabited. I was told that it was haunted, that no one would inhabit it. I smiled at what seemed to me so idle a story. I spent more money in repairing it – added to its old-fashioned furniture a few modern articles – advertised it, and obtained a lodger for a year. He was a colonel on half-pay. He came in with his family, a son and a daughter, and four or five servants: they all left the house the next day; and, although each of them declared that he had seen something different from that which had scared the others, a something still was equally terrible to all. I really could not in conscience sue, nor even blame, the colonel for breach of agreement. Then I put in the old woman I have spoken of, and she was empowered to let the house in apartments. I never had one lodger who stayed more than three days. I do not tell you their stories – to no two lodgers have there been exactly the same phenomena repeated. It is better that you should judge for yourself, than enter the house with an imagination influenced by previous narratives; only be prepared to see and hear something or other, and take whatever precautions you yourself please.'

'Have you never had a curiosity yourself to pass a night in that house?'

'Yes, I passed not a night, but three hours in broad daylight in that house. My curiosity is not satisfied, but is quenched. I have no desire to renew the experiment. You cannot complain, you see, sir, that I am not sufficiently candid; and unless your interest be exceedingly eager and your nerves unusually strong, I honestly add, that I advise you *not* to pass a night in that house.'

'My interest *is* exceedingly keen,' said I, 'and though only a coward will boast of his nerves in situations wholly unfamiliar to him, yet my nerves have been seasoned in such variety of danger that I have the right to rely on them – even in a haunted house.'

Mr J – said very little more; he took the keys of the house out of his bureau, gave them to me – and, thanking him cordially for his frankness, and his urbane concession to my wish, I carried off my prize.

Impatient for the experiment, as soon as I reached home, I summoned my confidential servant – a young man of gay spirits, fearless temper, and as free from superstitious prejudice as anyone I could think of.

'F – ,' said I, 'you remember in Germany how disappointed we were at not finding a ghost in that old castle, which was said to be haunted by a headless apparition? Well, I have heard of a house in London which, I have reason to hope, is decidedly haunted. I mean to sleep there tonight. From what I hear, there is no doubt that something will allow itself to be seen or to be heard – something, perhaps, excessively horrible. Do you think, if I take you with me, I may rely on your presence of mind, whatever may happen?'

'Oh, sir! pray trust me,' answered F – , grinning with delight.

'Very well; then here are the keys of the house – this is the address. Go now – select for me any bedroom you please; and since the house has not been inhabited for weeks, make up a good fire – air the bed well – see, of course, that there are candles as well as fuel. Take with you my revolver and my dagger – so much for my weapons – arm yourself equally well; and if we are not a match for a dozen ghosts, we shall be but a sorry couple of Englishmen.'

I was engaged for the rest of the day on business so urgent that I had no leisure to think much on the nocturnal adventure to which I had plighted my honour. I dined alone, and very late, and while dining, read, as is my habit. I selected one of the volumes of Macaulay's essays. I thought to myself that I would take the book with me; there was so much of healthfulness in the style, and practical life in the subjects, that it would serve as an antidote against the influences of superstitious fancy.

Accordingly, about half-past nine, I put the book into my pocket, and strolled leisurely towards the haunted house. I took with me a favourite dog – an exceedingly sharp, bold, and vigilant bull-terrier – a dog fond of prowling about strange ghostly corners and passages at night in search of rats – a dog of dogs for a ghost.

It was a summer night, but chilly, the sky somewhat gloomy and overcast. Still there was a moon – faint and sickly, but still a moon – and if the clouds permitted, after midnight it would be brighter.

I reached the house, knocked, and my servant opened with a cheerful smile.

'All right, sir, and very comfortable.'

'Oh!' said I, rather disappointed; 'have you not seen or heard anything remarkable?'

'Well, sir, I must own I have heard something queer.'

'What? – what?'

'The sound of feet pattering behind me; and once or twice small noises like whispers close at my ear – nothing more.'

'You are not at all frightened?'

'I! not a bit of it, sir,' and the man's bold look reassured me on one point – viz., that happen what might, he would not desert me.

We were in the hall, the street-door closed, and my attention was now drawn to my dog. He had at first run in eagerly enough, but had sneaked back to the door, and was scratching and whining to get out. After patting him on the head, and encouraging him gently, the dog seemed to reconcile himself to the situation, and followed me and F – through the house, but keeping close at my heels instead of hurrying inquisitively in advance, which was his usual and normal habit in all strange places. We first visited the subterranean apartments, the kitchen and other offices, and especially the cellars, in which last there were two or three bottles of wine still left in the bin, covered with cobwebs, and evidently, by their appearance, undisturbed for many years. It was clear that the ghosts were not wine-bibbers. For the rest we discovered nothing of interest. There was a gloomy little backyard, with very high walls. The stones of this yard were very damp; and what with the damp, and what with the dust and smoke-grime on the pavement, our feet left a slight impression where we passed. And now appeared the first strange phenomenon witnessed by myself in this strange abode. I saw, just before me, the print of a foot suddenly form itself, as it were. I stopped, caught hold of my servant, and pointed to it. In advance of that footprint as suddenly dropped another. We both saw it. I advanced quickly to the place; the footprints kept advancing before me, a small footprint – the foot of a child: the impression was too faint thoroughly to distinguish the shape, but it seemed to us both that it was the print of a naked foot. This phenomenon ceased when we arrived at the opposite wall, nor did it repeat itself on returning. We remounted the stairs, and entered the rooms on the ground floor, a dining parlour, a small back-parlour, and a still smaller third room that had been probably appropriated to a footman – all still as death. We then visited the drawing-rooms, which seemed fresh and new. In the front room I seated myself in an arm- chair. F – placed on the table the candle-stick with which he had lighted us. I told him to shut the door. As he turned to do so, a chair opposite to me moved from the wall quickly and noiselessly, and dropped itself about a yard from my own chair, immediately fronting it.

'Why, this is better than the turning tables,' said I, with a half-laugh; and as I laughed, my dog put back his head and howled.

F – , coming back, had not observed the movement of the chair. He employed himself now in stilling the dog. I continued to gaze on the chair, and fancied I saw on it a pale blue misty outline of a human figure, but an outline so indistinct that I could only distrust my own vision. The dog was now quiet.

'Put back that chair opposite to me,' said I to F – ; 'put it back to the wall.'

F – obeyed. 'Was that you, sir,' said he, turning abruptly.

'I! – what?'

'Why, something struck me. I felt it sharply on the shoulder – just here.'

'No,' said I. 'But we have jugglers present, and though we may not discover their tricks, we shall catch *them* before they frighten *us*.'

We did not stay long in the drawing-rooms – in fact, they felt so damp and so chilly that I was glad to get to the fire upstairs. We locked the doors of the drawing-rooms – a precaution which, I should observe, we had taken with all the rooms we had searched below. The bedroom my servant had selected for me was the best on the floor – a large one, with two windows fronting the street. The four-posted bed, which took up no inconsiderable space, was opposite to the fire, which burnt clear and bright; a door in the wall to the left, between the bed and the window, communicated with the room which my servant appropriated to himself. This last was a small room with a sofa-bed, and had no communication with the landing-place – no other door but that which conducted to the bedroom I was to occupy. On either side of my fireplace was a cupboard, without locks, flush with the wall, and covered with the same dull-brown paper. We examined these cupboards – only hooks to suspend female dresses – nothing else; we sounded the walls – evidently solid – the outer walls of the building. Having finished the survey of these apartments, warmed myself a few moments, and lighted my cigar, I then, still accompanied by F – , went forth to complete my reconnoitre. In the landing-place there was another door; it was closed firmly. 'Sir,' said my servant, in surprise, 'I unlocked this door with all the others when I first came; it cannot have got locked from the inside, for – '

Before he had finished his sentence, the door, which neither of us then was touching, opened quietly of itself. We looked at each other a single instant. The same thought seized both – some human agency might be detected here. I rushed in first, my servant followed. A small, blank, dreary room without furniture – a few empty boxes and hampers in a corner – a small window – the shutters closed – not even a fireplace – no other door but that by which we had entered – no carpet on the floor, and the floor seemed very old, uneven, worm-eaten, mended here and there, as was shown by the whiter patches on the woods; but no living being, and no visible place in which a living being could have hidden. As we stood gazing round, the door by which we had entered closed as quietly as it had before opened: we were imprisoned.

For the first time I felt a creep of undefinable horror. Not so my servant. 'Why, they don't think to trap us, sir; I could break that trumpery door with a kick of my foot.'

'Try first if it will open to your hand,' said I, shaking off the vague apprehension that had seized me, 'while I unclose the shutters and see what is without.'

I unbarred the shutters – the window looked on the little backyard I have before described; there was no ledge without – nothing to break the sheer descent of the wall. No man getting out of that window would have found any footing till he had fallen on the stones below.

F – , meanwhile, was vainly attempting to open the door. He now turned round to me and asked my permission to use force. And I should here state, in justice to the servant, that, far from evincing any superstitious terrors, his nerve, composure, and even gaiety amidst circumstances so extraordinary, compelled my admiration, and made me congratulate myself on having secured a companion in every way fitted to the occasion. I willingly gave him the permission he required. But though he was a remarkably strong man, his force was as idle as his milder efforts; the door did not even shake to his stoutest kick. Breathless and panting, he desisted. I then tried the door myself, equally in vain. As I ceased from the effort, again that creep of horror came over me; but this time it was more cold and stubborn. I felt as if some strange and ghastly exhalation were rising up from the chinks of that rugged floor, and filling the atmosphere with a venomous influence hostile to human life. The door now very slowly and quietly opened as of its own accord. We precipitated ourselves into the landing-place. We both saw a large pale light – as large as the human figure, but shapeless and unsubstantial – move before us, and ascend the stairs that led from the landing into the attics. I followed the light, and my servant followed me. It entered to the right of the landing a small garret, of which the door stood open. I entered in the same instant. The light then collapsed into a small globule, exceedingly brilliant and vivid: rested a moment on a bed in the corner, quivered, and vanished. We approached the bed and examined it – a half-tester, such as is commonly found in attics devoted to servants. On the drawers that stood near it we perceived an old faded silk kerchief, with the needle still left in a rent half repaired. The kerchief was covered with dust; probably it had belonged to the old woman who had last died in that house, and this might have been her sleeping-room. I had sufficient curiosity to open the drawers: there were a few odds and ends of female dress, and two letters tied round with a narrow ribbon of faded yellow. I took the liberty to possess myself of the letters. We found nothing else in the room worth noticing – nor did the light reappear; but we distinctly heard, as we turned to go, a pattering footfall on the floor – just before us. We went through the other attics (in all four), the footfall still preceding us. Nothing to be seen – nothing but the footfall heard. I had the letters in my hand: just as I was descending the stairs I distinctly felt my wrist seized, and a faint soft effort made to draw the letters from my clasp. I only held them the more tightly, and the effort ceased.

We regained the bed-chamber appropriated to myself, and I then remarked that my dog had not followed us when we had left it. He was thrusting himself close to the fire, and trembling. I was impatient to examine the letters; and while I read them, my servant opened a little box in which he had deposited the weapons I had ordered him to bring; took them out, placed them on a table close at my bed-head, and then occupied himself in soothing the dog, who, however, seemed to heed him very little.

The letters were short – they were dated; the dates exactly thirty-five years ago. They were evidently from a lover to his mistress, or a husband to some young wife.

Not only the terms of expression, but a distinct reference to a former voyage, indicated the writer to have been a seafarer. The spelling and hand-writing were those of a man imperfectly educated, but still the language itself was forcible. In the expressions of endearment there was a kind of rough, wild love; but here and there were dark, unintelligible hints at some secret not of love – some secret that seemed of crime. 'We ought to love each other,' was one of the sentences I remember, 'for how everyone else would execrate us if all was known.' Again: 'Don't let anyone be in the same room with you at night – you talk in your sleep.' And again: 'What's done can't be undone; and I tell you there's nothing against us unless the dead could come to life.' Here there was underlined in a better handwriting (a female's), 'They do!' At the end of the letter latest in date the same female hand had written these words: 'Lost at sea the 4th of June, the same day as – .'

I put down the letters, and began to muse over their contents. Fearing, however that the train of thought into which I fell might unsteady my nerves, I fully determined to keep my mind in a fit state to cope with whatever of the Marvellous the advancing night might bring forth. I roused myself – laid the letters on the table – stirred up the fire, which was still bright and cheering, and opened my volume of Macaulay. I read quietly enough till about half past eleven. I then threw myself dressed upon the bed, and told my servant he might retire to his own room, but must keep himself awake. I bade him leave open the door between the two rooms. Thus alone, I kept two candles burning on the table by my bed-head. I placed my watch beside the weapons, and calmly resumed my Macaulay. Opposite to me the fire burned clear; and on the hearth-rug, seemingly asleep, lay the dog. In about twenty minutes I felt an exceedingly cold air pass my cheek, like a sudden draught. I fancied the door to my right, communicating with the landing-place, must have got open; but no – it was closed. I then turned my glance to my left, and saw the flame of the candles violently swayed as by a wind. At the same moment the watch beside the revolver softly slid from the table – softly, softly – no visible hand – it was gone. I sprang up, seizing the revolver with the one hand, the dagger with the other: I was not willing that my weapons should share the fate of the watch. Thus armed, I looked round the floor – no sign of the watch. Three slow, loud, distinct knocks were now heard at the bed-head; my servant called out, 'Is that you, sir?'

'No; be on your guard.'

The dog now roused himself and sat on his haunches, his ears moving quickly backwards and forwards. He kept his eyes fixed on me with a look so strange that he concentrated all my attention on himself. Slowly, he rose up, all his hair bristling, and stood perfectly rigid, and with the same wild stare. I had no time, however, to examine the dog. Presently my servant emerged from his room; and if ever I saw horror in the human face, it was then.

I should not have recognized him had we met in the street, so altered was every lineament. He passed by me quickly, saying in a whisper that seemed scarcely to come from his lips, 'Run-run! it is after me!' He gained the door to the landing, pulled it open, and rushed forth. I followed him into the landing involuntarily, calling him to stop; but, without heeding me, he bounded down the stairs, clinging to the balusters, and taking several steps at a time. I heard, where I stood, the street door open – heard it again clap to. I was left alone in the haunted house.

It was but for a moment that I remained undecided whether or not to follow my servant; pride and curiosity alike forbade so dastardly a flight. I re-entered my room, closing the door after me, and proceeded cautiously into the interior chamber. I encountered nothing to justify my servant's terror. I again carefully examined the walls, to see if there were any concealed door. I could find no trace of one – not even a seam in the dull-brown paper with which the room was hung. How, then, had the THING, whatever it was, which had so scared him, obtained ingress except through my own chamber? I returned to my room, shut and locked the door that opened upon the interior one, and stood on the hearth, expectant and prepared. I now perceived that the dog had slunk into an angle of the wall, and was pressing himself close against it, as if literally striving to force his way into it. I approached the animal and spoke to it; the poor brute was evidently beside itself with terror. It showed all its teeth, the slaver dropped from its jaws, and would certainly have bitten me if I had touched it. It did not seem to recognize me. Whoever has seen at the Zoological Gardens a rabbit, fascinated by a serpent, cowering in a corner, may form some idea of the anguish which the dog exhibited. Finding all efforts to soothe the animal in vain, and fearing that his bite might be as venomous in that state as in the madness of a hydrophobia, I left him alone, placed my weapons on the table beside the fire, seated myself, and recommenced my Macaulay.

Perhaps, in order not to appear seeking credit for a courage, or rather a coolness which the reader may conceive I exaggerate, I may be pardoned if I pause to indulge in one or two egotistical remarks.

As I hold presence of mind, or what is called courage, to be precisely proportioned to familiarity with the circumstances that lead to it, so I should say that I had been long sufficiently familiar with all experiments that appertain to the Marvellous. I had witnessed many very extraordinary phenomena in various parts of the world – phenomena that would be either totally disbelieved if I stated them, or ascribed to supernatural agencies. Now, my theory is that the Supernatural is the Impossible, and that what is called supernatural is only a something in the laws of nature of which we have been hitherto ignorant. Therefore, if a ghost rises before me, I have not the right to say, 'So, then, the supernatural is possible', but rather, 'So, then, the apparition of a ghost is, contrary to received opinion, within the laws of nature – i.e., not supernatural'.

Now, in all that I hitherto witnessed, and indeed in all the wonders which the amateurs of mystery in our age record as facts, a material living agency is always required. On the Continent you will find still magicians who assert that they can raise spirits. Assume for the moment that they assert truly, still the living material form of the magician is present; and he is the material agency by which, from some constitutional peculiarities, certain strange phenomena are represented to your natural senses.

Accept, again, as truthful, the tales of Spirit Manifestation in America – musical or other sounds – writings on paper, produced by no discernible hand – articles of furniture moved without apparent human agency – or the actual sight and touch of hands, to which no bodies seem to belong – still there must be found the MEDIUM of living being, with constitutional peculiarities capable of obtaining these signs. In fine, in all such marvels, supposing even that there is no imposture, there must be a human being like ourselves by whom, or through whom, the effects presented to human beings are produced. It is so with the now familiar phenomena of mesmerism or electro-biology; the mind of the person operated on is affected through a material living agent. Nor, supposing it true that a mesmerized patient can respond to the will or passes of a mesmerizer a hundred miles distant, is the response less occasioned by a material being; it may be through a material fluid – call it Electric, call it Odic, call it what you will – which has the power of traversing space and passing obstacles, that the material effect is communicated from one to the other. Hence all that I had hitherto witnessed, or expected to witness, in this strange house, I believed to be occasioned through some agency or medium as mortal as myself; and this idea necessarily prevented the awe with which those who regard as supernatural things that are not within the ordinary operations of nature, might have been impressed by the adventures of that memorable night.

As, then, it was my conjecture that all that was presented, or would be presented to my senses, must originate in some human being gifted by constitution with the power so to present them, and having some motive so to do, I felt an interest in my theory which, in its way, was rather philosophical than superstitious. And I can sincerely say that I was in as tranquil a temper for observation as any practical experimentalist could be in awaiting the effects of some rare, though perhaps perilous, chemical combination. Of course, the more I kept my mind detached from fancy, the more the temper fitted for observation would be obtained; and I therefore riveted eye and thought on the strong daylight sense in the page of my Macaulay.

I now became aware that something interposed between the page and the light – the page was overshadowed: I looked up, and I saw what I shall find it very difficult, perhaps impossible, to describe.

It was Darkness shaping itself forth from the air in very undefined outline. I cannot say it was of a human form, and yet it had more resemblance to a human form, or rather shadow, than to anything else. As it stood, wholly apart and distinct from the air and the light around it, its dimensions seemed gigantic, the summit nearly touching the ceiling. While I gazed, a feeling of intense cold seized me. An iceberg before me could not more have chilled me; nor could the cold of an iceberg have been more purely physical. I feel convinced that it was not the cold caused by fear. As I continued to gaze, I thought – but this I cannot say with precision – that I distinguished two eyes looking down on me from the height. One moment I fancied that I distinguished them clearly, the next they seemed gone; but still two rays of a pale-blue light frequently shot through the darkness, as from the height on which I half believed half doubted, that I had encountered the eyes.

I strove to speak – my voice utterly failed me; I could only think to myself, 'Is this fear? it is *not* fear!' I strove to rise – in vain; I felt as if weighed down by an irresistible force. Indeed, my impression was that of an immense and overwhelming Power opposed to my volition; that sense of utter inadequacy to cope with a force beyond men's, which one may feel *physically* in a storm at sea, in a conflagration, or when confronting some terrible wild beast, or rather, perhaps, the shark of the ocean, I felt *morally*. Opposed to my will was another will, as far superior to its strength as storm, fire, and shark are superior in material force to the force of man.

And now, as this impression grew on me – now came, at last, horror – horror to a degree that no words can convey. Still I retained pride, if not courage; and in my own mind I said: 'This is horror, but it is not fear; unless I fear I cannot be harmed; my reason rejects this thing; it is an illusion – I do not fear.' With a violent effort I succeeded at last in stretching out my hand towards the weapon on the table: as I did so, on the arm and shoulder I received a strange shock, and my arm fell to my side powerless. And now, to add to my horror, the light began slowly to wane from the candles – they were not, as it were, extinguished, but their flame seemed very gradually withdrawn: it was the same with the fire – the light extracted from the fuel; in a few minutes the room was in utter darkness. The dread that came over me, to be thus in the dark with that dark Thing, whose power was so intensely felt, brought a reaction of nerve. In fact, terror had reached that climax, that either my senses must have deserted me, or I must have burst through the spell. I did burst through it. I found voice, though the voice was a shriek. I remember that I broke forth with words like these: 'I do not fear, my soul does not fear'; and at the same time I found strength to rise. Still in that profound gloom I rushed to one of the windows – tore aside the curtain – flung open the shutters; my first thought was – LIGHT. And when I saw the moon high, clear, and calm, I felt a joy that almost compensated for the previous terror. There was the moon, there was also the light from the gas-lamps in the deserted slumberous street. I turned to look back into the room; the moon penetrated its shadow very palely and partially – but still there was light. The dark Thing, whatever it might be, was gone – except that I could yet see a dim shadow, which seemed the shadow of that shade, against the opposite wall.

My eye now rested on the table, and from under the table (which was without cloth or cover – an old mahogany round table) there rose a Hand, visible as far as the wrist. It was a hand, seemingly, as much of flesh and blood as my own, but the hand of an aged person – lean, wrinkled, small too – a woman's hand. That hand very softly closed on the two letters that lay on the table: hand and letters both vanished. There then came the same three loud measured knocks I had heard at the bed-head before this extraordinary drama had commenced.

As those sounds slowly ceased, I felt the whole room vibrate sensibly; and at the far end there rose, as from the floor, sparks or globules like bubbles of light, many-coloured – green, yellow, fire-red, azure. Up and down, to and fro, hither, as tiny will-o'-the-wisps, the sparks moved, slow or swift, each at its own caprice. A chair (as in the drawing-room below) was now advanced from the wall without apparent agency, and placed at the opposite side of the table. Suddenly, as forth from the chair, there grew a shape – a woman's shape. It was distinct as a shape of life – ghastly as a shape of death. The face was that of youth, with a strange mournful beauty; the throat and shoulders were bare, the rest of the form in a loose robe of cloudy white. It began sleeking its long yellow hair, which fell over its shoulders; its eyes were not turned towards me, but to the door; it seemed listening, watching, waiting. The shadow of the shade in the background grew darker; and again I thought I beheld the eyes gleaming out from the summit of the shadow – eyes fixed upon that shape.

As if from the door, as though it did not open, there grew out another shape, equally distinct, equally ghastly – a man's shape – a young man's. It was in the dress of the last century, or rather in a likeness of such dress (for both the male shape and the female, though defined, were evidently unsubstantial, impalpable – simulacra – phantasms); and there was something incongruous, grotesque, yet fearful, in the contrast between the elaborate finery, the courtly precision of that old-fashioned garb, with its ruffles and lace and buckles, and the corpse-like aspect and ghost-like stillness of the flitting wearer. Just as the male shape approached the female, the dark Shadow started from the wall, all three for a moment wrapped in darkness. When the pale light returned, the two phantoms were as if in the grasp of the Shadow that towered between them; and there was a blood-stain on the breast of the female; and the phantom male was leaning on its phantom sword, and blood seemed trickling fast from the ruffles, from the lace; and the darkness of the intermediate Shadow swallowed them up – they were gone. And again the bubbles of light shot, and sailed, and undulated, growing thicker and thicker and more wildly confused in their movements.

The closet door to the right of the fireplace now opened, and from the aperture there came the form of an aged woman. In her hand she held letters – the very letters over which I had seen *the* Hand close; and behind her I heard a footstep. She turned round as if to listen, and then she opened the letters and seemed to read; and over her shoulder I saw a livid face, the face as of a man long drowned – bloated, bleached – seaweed tangled in its dripping hair; and at her feet lay a form as of a corpse, and beside the corpse there cowered a child, a miserable squalid child, with famine in its cheeks and fear in its eyes. And as I looked in the old woman's face, the wrinkles and lines vanished, and it became a face of youth – hard-eyed, stony, but still youth; and the Shadow darted forth, and darkened over those phantoms as it had darkened over the last.

Nothing now was left but the Shadow, and on that my eyes were intently fixed, till again eyes grew out of the Shadow – malignant, serpent eyes. And the bubbles of light again rose and fell, and in their disordered, irregular, turbulent maze, mingled with the wan moonlight. And now from these globules themselves, as from the shell of an egg, monstrous things burst out; the air grew filled with them; larvae so bloodless and so hideous that I can in no way describe them except to remind the reader of the swarming life which a solar microscope brings before his eyes in a drop of water – things transparent, supple, agile, chasing each other, devouring each other – forms like nought ever beheld by the naked eye. As the shapes were without symmetry, so their movements were without order. In their very vagrancies there was no sport; they came round me and round, thicker and faster and swifter, swarming over my head, crawling over my right arm, which was outstretched in involuntary command against all evil beings. Sometimes I felt myself touched, but not by them; invisible hands touched me. Once I felt the clutch as of cold, soft fingers at my throat. I was still equally conscious that if I gave way to fear I should be in bodily peril; and I concentrated all my faculties in the single focus of resisting, stubborn will. And I turned my sight from the Shadow – above all, from those strange serpent eyes – eyes that had now become distinctly visible. For there, though in nought else around me, I was aware that there was a Will, and a will of intense, creative, working evil, which might crush down my own.

The pale atmosphere in the room began now to redden as if in the air of some near conflagration. The larvae grew lurid as things that live in fire. Again the room vibrated; again were heard the three measured knocks; and again all things were swallowed up in the darkness of the dark Shadow, as if out of that darkness all had come, into that darkness all returned.

As the gloom receded, the Shadow was wholly gone. Slowly, as it had been withdrawn, the flame grew again into the candles on the table, again into the fuel in the grate. The whole room came once more calmly, healthfully into sight.

The two doors were still closed, the door communicating with the servant's room still locked. In the corner of the wall, into which he had so convulsively niched himself, lay the dog. I called to him – no movement; I approached – the animal was dead; his eyes protruded; his tongue out of his mouth; the froth gathered round his jaws. I took him in my arms; I brought him to the fire; I felt acute grief for the loss of my poor favourite – acute self-reproach; I accused myself of his death; I imagined he had died of fright. But what was my surprise on finding that his neck was actually broken. Had this been done in the dark? – must it not have been by a hand human as mine? – must there not have been a human agency all the while in that room? Good cause to suspect it. I cannot tell. I cannot do more than state the fact fairly; the reader may draw his own inference.

Another surprising circumstance – my watch was restored to the table from which it had been so mysteriously withdrawn; but it had stopped at the very moment it was so withdrawn; nor, despite all the skill of the watchmaker, has it ever gone since – that is, it will go in a strange erratic way for a few hours, and then come to a dead stop – it is worthless.

Nothing more chanced for the rest of the night. Nor, indeed, had I long to wait before the dawn broke. Nor till it was broad daylight did I quit the haunted house. Before I did so, I revisited the little blind room in which my servant and myself had been for a time imprisoned. I had a strong impression – for which I could not account – that from that room had originated the mechanism of the phenomena – if I may use the term – which had been experienced in my chamber. And though I entered it now in the clear day, with the sun peering through the filmy window, I still felt, as I stood on its floors, the creep of the horror which I had first there experienced the night before, and which had been so aggravated by what had passed in my own chamber. I could not, indeed, bear to stay more than half a minute within those walls. I descended the stairs, and again I heard the footfall before me; and when I opened the street door, I thought I could distinguish a very low laugh. I gained my own home, expecting to find my runaway servant there. But he had not presented himself, nor did I hear more of him for three days, when I received a letter from him, dated from Liverpool, to this effect:

Honoured Sir:

I humbly entreat your pardon, though I can scarcely hope that you will think that I deserve it, unless – which Heaven forbid! – you saw what I did. I feel it will be years before I can recover myself; and as to being fit for service, it is out of the question. I am therefore going to my brother-in-law at Melbourne. The ship sails tomorrow. Perhaps the long voyage may set me up. I do nothing now but start and tremble, and fancy IT is behind me. I humbly beg you, honoured sir, to order my clothes, and whatever wages are due to me, to be sent to my mother's, at Walworth – John knows her address.

The letter ended with additional apologies, somewhat incoherent, and explanatory details as to effect that had been under the writer's charge.

This flight may perhaps warrant a suspicion that the man wished to go to Australia, and had been somehow or other fraudulently mixed up with the events of the night. I say nothing in refutation of that conjecture; rather, I suggest it as one that would seem to many persons the most probable solution of improbable occurrences. My belief in my own theory remained unshaken. I returned in the evening to the house, to bring away in a hack cab the things I had left there, with my poor dog's body. In this task I was not disturbed, nor did any incident worth note befall me, except that still, on ascending and descending the stairs, I heard the same footfall in advance. On leaving the house, I went to Mr J – 's. He was at home. I returned him the keys, told him that my curiosity was sufficiently gratified, and was about to relate quickly what had passed, when he stopped me, and said, though with much politeness, that he had no longer any interest in a mystery which none had ever solved.

I determined at least to tell him of the two letters I had read, as well as of the extraordinary manner in which they had disappeared, and I then inquired if he thought they had been addressed to the woman who had died in the house, and if there were anything in her early history which could possibly confirm the dark suspicions to which the letters gave rise. Mr J – seemed startled, and, after musing a few moments, answered: 'I am but little acquainted with the woman's earlier history, except, as I before told you, that her family were known to mine. But you revive some vague reminiscences to her prejudice. I will make inquiries, and inform you of their result. Still, even if we could admit the popular superstition that a person who had been either the perpetrator or the victim of dark crimes in life could revisit, as a restless spirit, the scene in which those crimes had been committed, I should observe that the house was infested by strange sights and sounds before the old woman died – you smile – what would you say?'

'I would say this, that I am convinced, if we could get to the bottom of these mysteries, we should find a living human agency.'

'What! you believe it is all an imposture? for what object?'

'Not an imposture in the ordinary sense of the word. If suddenly I were to sink into a deep sleep, from which you could not awake me, but in that sleep could answer questions with an accuracy which I could not pretend to when awake – tell you what money you had in your pocket – nay, describe your very thoughts – it is not necessarily an imposture, any more than it is necessarily supernatural. I should be, unconsciously to myself, under a mesmeric influence, conveyed to me from a distance by a human being who had acquired power over me by previous *rapport*.'

'But if a mesmerizer could so affect another living being, can you suppose that a mesmerizer could also affect inanimate objects: move chairs – open and shut doors?'

'Or impress our senses with the belief in such effects – we never having been *en rapport* with the person acting on us? No. What is commonly called mesmerism could not do this; but there may be a power akin to mesmerism and superior to it – the power that in the old days was called Magic. That such a power may extend to all inanimate objects of matter, I do not say; but if so, it would not be against nature – it would only be a rare power in nature which might be given to constitutions with certain peculiarities, and cultivated by practise to an extraordinary degree. That such a power might extend over the dead – that is, over certain thoughts and memories that the dead may still retain – and compel, not that which ought properly to be called the SOUL, and which is far beyond human reach, but rather a phantom of what has been most earth-stained on earth to make itself apparent to our senses – is a very ancient though obsolete theory, upon which I will hazard no opinion. But I do not conceive the power would be supernatural. Let me illustrate what I mean from an experiment which Paracelsus describes as not difficult, and which the author of the *Curiosities of Literature* cites as credible: A flower perishes; you burn it. Whatever were the elements of that flower while it lived are gone, dispersed, you know not whither; you can never discover nor re-collect them. But you can, by chemistry, out of the burnt dust of that flower, raise a spectrum of the flower, just as it seemed in life. It may be the same with the human being. The soul has as much escaped you as the essence or elements of the flower. Still you may make a spectrum of it. And this phantom, through the popular superstition it is held to be the soul of the departed, must not be confounded with the true soul; it is but the eidolon of the dead form. Hence, like the best attested stories of ghosts or spirits, the thing that most strikes us is the absence of what we hold to be the soul; that is, of superior emancipation intelligence. These apparitions come for little or no object – they seldom speak when they do come; if they speak, they utter no ideas above those of an ordinary person on earth, they utter no ideas above those of an ordinary person on earth. American spirit-seers have published volumes of communications, in prose and verse, which they assert to be given in the names of the most illustrious dead – Shakespeare, Bacon – Heaven knows whom. Those communications, taking the best, are certainly not a whit of higher order than would be communications from living persons of fair talent and education; they are wondrously inferior to what Bacon, Shakespeare, and Plato said and wrote when on earth. Nor, what is more noticeable, do they ever contain an idea that was not on earth before. Wonderful, therefore, as such phenomena may be (granting them to be truthful), I see much that philosophy may question, nothing that it is incumbent on philosophy to deny – viz., nothing supernatural. They are but ideas conveyed somehow or other (we have not yet discovered the means) from one mortal brain to another. Whether, in so doing, tables walk of their own accord, or fiend-like shapes appear in a magic circle, or bodyless hands rise and remove material objects, or a Thing of Darkness, such as presented itself to me, freeze our blood – still am I persuaded that these are but agencies conveyed, as by electric wires, to my own brain from the brain of another. In some constitutions there is a natural chemistry, and those constitutions may produce chemic wonders – in others a natural fluid, call it electricity, and these may produce electric wonders. But the wonders differ from Normal Science in this – they are alike objectless, purposeless, puerile, frivolous. They lead on to no grand results, and therefore the world does not heed, and true sages have not cultivated them. But sure I am, that of all I saw or heard, a man, human as myself, was the remote originator; and I believe unconsciously to himself as to the exact effects produced, for this reason: no two persons, you say, have ever told you that they experienced exactly the same thing. Well, observe, no two persons ever experienced exactly the same dream. If this were an ordinary imposture, the machinery would be arranged for results that would but little vary; if it were a super-natural agency permitted by the Almighty, it would surely be for some definite end. These phenomena belong to neither class; my persuasion is that they originate in some brain now far distant; that that brain had no distinct volition in anything that occurred; that what does occur reflects but its devious, motley, ever-shifting, half-formed thoughts; in short, that it has been but the dreams of such a brain put into action and invested with a semi-substance. That this brain is of immense power, that it can set matter into movement, that it is malignant and destructive, I believe; some material force must have killed my dog; the same force might, for aught I know, have sufficed to kill myself, had I been as subjugated by terror as the dog – had my intellect or my spirit given me no countervailing resistance in my will.'

'It killed your dog! that is fearful! indeed it is strange that no animal can be induced to stay in that house; not even a cat. Rats and mice are never found in it.'

'The instincts of the brute creation detect influences deadly to their existence. Man's reason has a sense less subtle, because it has a resisting power more supreme. But enough; do you comprehend my theory?'

'Yes, though imperfectly – and I accept any crotchet (pardon the word), however odd, rather than embrace at once the notion of ghosts and hobgoblins we imbibed in our nurseries. Still, to my unfortunate house the evil is the same. What on earth can I do with the house?'

'I will tell you what I would do. I am convinced from my own internal feelings that the small unfurnished room at right angles to the door of the bedroom which I occupied forms a starting-point or receptacle for the influences which haunt the house; and I strongly advise you to have the walls opened, the floor removed – nay, the whole room pulled down. I observe that it is detached from the body of the house, built over the small back-yard, and could be removed without injury to the rest of the building.'

'And you think, if I did that – '

'You would cut off the telegraph wires. Try it. I am so persuaded that I am right, that I will pay half the expense if you will allow me to direct the operations.'

'Nay, I am well able to afford the cost; for the rest, allow me to write to you.'

About ten days after, I received a letter from Mr J – , telling me that he had visited the house since I had seen him; that he had found the two letters I had described, replaced in the drawer from which I had taken them; that he had read them with misgivings like my own; that he had instituted a cautious inquiry about the woman to whom I rigidly conjectured they had been written. It seemed that thirty-six years ago (a year before the date of the letters) she had married, against the wish of her relations, an American of very suspicious character; in fact, he was generally believed to have been a pirate. She herself was the daughter of very respectable tradespeople, and had served in the capacity of a nursery governess before her marriage. She had a brother, a widower, who was considered wealthy, and who had one child of about six years old. A month after the marriage, the body of this brother was found in the Thames, near London Bridge; there seemed some marks of violence about his throat, but they were not deemed sufficient to warrant the inquest in any other verdict than that of 'found drowned'.

The American and his wife took charge of the little boy, the deceased brother having by his will left his sister the guardian of his only child – and in the event of the child's death, the sister inherited. The child died about six months afterwards – it was supposed to have been neglected and ill-treated. The neighbours deposed to have heard it shriek at night. The surgeon who had examined it after death said that it was emaciated as if from want of nourishment, and the body was covered with livid bruises. It seemed that one winter night the child had sought to escape – crept out into the backyard – tried to scale the wall – fallen back exhausted, and been found at morning on the stones in a dying state. But though there was some evidence of cruelty, there was none of murder; and the aunt and her husband had sought to palliate cruelty by alleging the exceeding stubbornness and perversity of the child, who was declared to be half-witted. Be that as it may, at the orphan's death the aunt inherited her brother's fortune. Before the first wedded year was out, the American quitted England abruptly, and never returned to it. He obtained a cruising vessel, which was lost in the Atlantic two years afterwards. The widow was left in affluence: but reverses of various kinds had befallen her: a bank broke – an investment failed – she went into a small business and became insolvent – then she entered into service, sinking lower and lower, from housekeeper down to maid-of-all-work – never long retaining a place, though nothing decided against her character was ever alleged. She was considered sober, honest, and peculiarly quiet in her ways; still nothing prospered with her. And so she had dropped into the workhouse, from which Mr J – had taken her, to be placed in charge of the very house which she had rented as mistress in the first year of her wedded life.

Mr J – added that he had passed an hour alone in the unfurnished room which I had urged him to destroy, and that his impressions of dread while there were so great, though he had neither heard nor seen anything, that he was eager to have the walls bared and the floors removed as I had suggested. He had engaged persons for the work, and would commence any day I would name.

The day was accordingly fixed. I repaired to the haunted house – we went into the blind, dreary room, took up the skirting, and then the floors. Under the rafters, covered with rubbish, was found a trap-door, quite large enough to admit a man. It was closely nailed down, with clamps and rivets of iron. On removing these we descended into a room below, the existence of which has never been suspected. In this room there had been a window and a flue, but they had been bricked over, evidently for many years. By the help of candles we examined this place; it still retained some mouldering furniture – three chairs, an oak settle, a table – all of the fashion of about eighty years ago. There was a chest of drawers against the wall, in which we found, half-rotted away, old-fashioned articles of a man's dress, such as might have been worn eighty or a hundred years ago by a gentleman of some rank – costly steel buckles and buttons, like those yet worn in court dresses, a handsome court sword. In a waistcoat which had once been rich with gold lace, but which was now blackened and foul with damp, we found five guineas, a few silver coins, and an ivory ticket, probably for some place of entertainment long since passed away. But our main discovery was in a kind of iron safe fixed to the wall, the lock of which it cost us much trouble to get picked.

In this safe were three shelves, and two small drawers. Ranged on the shelves were several small bottles of crystal, hermetically stopped. They contained colourless volatile essences, of the nature of which I shall only say that they were not poisons – phosphor and ammonia entered into some of them. There were also some very curious glass tubes, and a small pointed rod of iron, with a large lump of rock-crystal, and another of amber – also a loadstone of great power.

In one of the drawers we found a miniature portrait set in gold, and retaining the freshness of its colours most remarkably, considering the length of time it had probably been there. The portrait was that of a man who might be somewhat advanced in middle life, perhaps forty-seven or forty-eight.

It was a remarkable face – a most impressive face. If you could fancy some mighty serpent transformed into man, preserving in the human lineaments the old servant type, you would have a better idea of that countenance than long descriptions can convey: the width and flatness of frontal – the tapering elegance of contour disguising the strength of the deadly jaw – the long, large, terrible eye, glittering and green as the emerald – and withal a certain ruthless calm, as if from the consciousness of an immense power.

Mechanically I turned round the miniature to examine the back of it, and on the back was engraved a pentacle; in the middle of the pentacle a ladder, and the third step of the ladder was formed by the date 1765. Examining still more minutely, I detected a spring; this, on being pressed, opened the back of the miniature as a lid. Withinside the lid was engraved 'Marianna to thee – Be faithful in life and in death to – .' Here follows a name that I will not mention, but it was not unfamiliar to me. I had heard it spoken of by old men in my childhood as the name borne by a dazzling charlatan who had made a great sensation in London for a year or so, and had fled the country on the charge of a double murder within his own house – that of his mistress and his rival. I said nothing of this to Mr J – , to whom reluctantly I resigned the miniature.

We had found no difficulty in opening the first drawer within the iron safe; we found great difficulty in opening the second: it was not locked, but it resisted all efforts, till we inserted in the chinks the edge of a chisel. When we had thus drawn it forth, we found a very singular apparatus in the nicest order. Upon a small thin book, or rather tablet, was placed a saucer of crystal; this saucer was filled with a clear liquid – on that liquid floated a kind of compass, with a needle shifting rapidly round; but instead of the usual points of a compass were seven strange characters, not very unlike those used by astrologers to denote the planets. A peculiar, but not strong nor displeasing odour, came from this drawer, which was lined with a wood that we afterwards discovered to be hazel. Whatever the cause of this odour, it produced a material effect on the nerves. We all felt it, even the two workmen who were in the room – a creeping tingling sensation from the tips of the fingers to the roots of the hair. Impatient to examine the tablet, I removed the saucer. As I did so the needle of the compass went round and round with exceeding swiftness, and I felt a shock that ran through my whole frame, so that I dropped the saucer on the floor. The liquid was spilt – the saucer was broken – the compass rolled to the end of the room – and at that instant the walls shook to and fro, as if a giant had swayed and rocked them.

The two workmen were so frightened that they ran up the ladder by which we had descended from the trap-door; but seeing that nothing more happened, they were easily induced to return.

Meanwhile I had opened the tablet: it was bound in plain red leather, with a silver clasp; it contained but one sheet of thick vellum, and on that sheet were inscribed, within a double pentacle, words in old monkish Latin, which are literally to be translated thus: 'On all that it can reach within these walls – sentient or inanimate, living or dead – as moves the needle, so work my will! Accursed be the house, and restless be the dwellers therein.'

We found no more. Mr J – burnt the tablet and its anathema. He razed to the foundations the part of the building containing the secret room with the chamber over it. He had then the courage to inhabit the house himself for a month, and a quieter, better-conditioned house could not be found in all London. Subsequently he let it to advantage, and his tenant has made no complaints.

The 'Ouanga' Charm

W. B. Seabrook

'Go bring me a humming bird,' said Maman Célie, 'and we'll see what can be done.'

She was talking to her tall grandson, Paul, Emanuel's boy, who had been moping about the habitation for days because a young, high-breasted black damsel down by the spring, who seemed to him more desirable than all the other young black damsels on the mountain, had tossed her crinkly head and sent him about his business.

It was through this idyllic episode of the humming bird that I discovered Maman Célie to be a sorceress, as well as a priestess of Voodoo. The two functions do not necessarily concur.

It seemed to me, however, that she had set her grandson a somewhat difficult task. I had seen humming birds occasionally down yonder among the tropical flowers and fig-banana groves, tiny, fragile, iridescent, darting sprites, as incorporeal as soap-bubbles, as swift to disappear at a threatened touch. To catch one of them seemed almost as difficult as trapping a sunbeam. I knew vaguely that naturalists made use of delicate and cunningly constructed nets, and I had heard with equal vagueness of tiny shotguns spraying microscopic pellets, but Paul was equipped only with his natural wits.

Next day he returned with the humming bird. He had trapped it with a sort of birdlime made of a sticky, gummy sap. It was already dead and Maman Célie hung it up to dry in the sunshine. Meanwhile she persuaded Paul to show me, reluctantly, a former love-charm she had fabricated for him, but which apparently had failed of its purpose, though he still wore it next to his skin in a little sack strung around his neck. She explained its construction and use. Two needles of equal length are stood upright, side by side, baptized with suitable incantations, and are given the names of the youth and his unwilling girl. The two in this particular case were called Paul and Ti-Marie. The needles are then left side by side, parallel but reversed, so that the point of each presses against the eye of the other. The point is symbolic of the phallus and the eye symbolic of the vulva. The reverse doubling simply increases the potency of the charm; it has no perverse significance. The needles are placed between twigs from the roots of the *bois chica* tree, whittled smooth and straight, and then wound round with thread. Like all charms of every sort in Haiti, it was called a *ouanga*. There are love-*ouangas*, hate-*ouangas*, birth-*ouangas*, protective-*ouangas*, and murder-*ouangas*. Sometimes they work, and sometimes they don't. Apparently this one hadn't worked, and Paul now centred all his hopes in the humming bird.

Aware of my curiosity about these matters, Maman Célie permitted me to see her make the new *ouanga*. It was a less weird, less cabalistic business than one might guess, though midnight and moonlight were in it, as she crouched, crooning her incantations, but there was nothing mysteriously dreadful. In a little wooden mortar, which they call *pilon*, she ground the dried body of the humming bird into a dustlike powder, droning, 'Wood of the woods, bird of the woods, woman you were created by God. Bird of the woods, fly into her heart. I command you in the name of the three Marys and in Ayida's name. *Dolor, Dolori, passa.*' There was much more of it, untranslatable and cryptic. And with the dried powder of the humming bird she mixed a few dried drops of her grandson's blood, also of his semen, likewise the pollen of jungle flowers.

When all this had been duly ground together into dustlike fineness, she transferred it to a leather pouch made (as Spanish shepherds often do to hold their love-charms) from the scrotum of a he-goat, and gave it to Paul next day.

I was told, for I did not see it, that on the following Saturday evening, at the *danse Congo*, as Ti-Marie swayed past him laughing, he threw the dust full in her face, and that half blinded, with the dust in her eyes and nostrils and mouth, she spat like a young wildcat, and cried out that she would kill him – but she lay with him that night in the forest, and on Monday morning he fetched her home. Doubtless a deeper magic than Maman Célie's was also at work, but I think it would be a mistake to assume *a priori* that without Maman Célie's incantations and the humming bird, Ti-Marie would have yielded.

There were two other occasions when I saw her magic work effectively. I saw her, by processes which she considered magical, cure a dying girl and catch a thief. She said and believed that it was magic. Words are merely labels, and we do not always explain the inner essence of things by rejecting the old labels and inventing new ones. The Lady of Shalott gazed in her crystal mirror to behold scenes far away, and that was sorcery; now we experiment with television, and that is science. The Witch of Endor was a witch, but Svengali is a hypnotist. Old Nostradamus working over his crucibles called it alchemy when he sought to transform lead to gold, but now the Germans are engaged in the same experiment and call it advanced chemistry. I realize that there is a flaw in these parallels. But the scientific-minded Carrel, after his long stay at Lourdes, came away convinced that there were invisible powers unknown to any science at work there, and that the probable power of immaterial emanations to produce constructive or destructive changes in material substances, for instance the human body, was a thing which saints still knew more about than savants. When such things occur at holy shrines, they are called miracles; when they occur in a psychological laboratory, they are called science; when they occur in the Haitian jungle, they are called Voodoo magic. These words are all tags, labels, nothing more. Life and the forces of life remain shrouded in eternal mystery.

Maman Célie's sorcery was principally benevolent, as when she presently began gathering materials for the construction of a *ouanga* packet for me – it seemed that I was to have one of my very own, like that of Louis, which was the first I had ever seen, down in my back yard at Port-au-Prince – and that it was to preserve me safe from all harm amid these mountains. It was to be used also, she told me, in the special ceremonial that would occur when I was finally led into the *houmfort* to face certain of the ultimate Voodoo mysteries. I would need it then, she assured me earnestly.

How much I believed in that *ouanga* packet, and in what manner I believed what I did believe, are questions difficult to answer. I suspect that generally in such matters it is easier to believe in things which are sinister, perhaps dangerous, than it is to believe in things which are benevolent. It is always easier to fear ghosts, hobgoblins, and demons than it is to feel the hovering presence of guardian spirits. How many millions of people have been terrorized by ghosts and sworn trembling afterwards to their reality, compared with the few score in the history of the world who, like Saint Augustine and Joan of Arc, have conversed with angels. I knew that certain other *ouanga* packets in this Voodoo sorcery, horridly devised, were sometimes as definitely deadly as the murderer's knife or poison. There is no question about that. Every white man who has lived long enough with primitive peoples, no matter what his hard scientific background, no matter how rational the texture of his mind, has come finally to an often reluctant admission of the fact. One may find the semi-scientific explanation of how so-called black magic can kill, in the fifteen volumes, more or less, of Frazer's *Golden Bough*; the condensed edition in two volumes has been emasculated. But if one has ever lived, I mean geographically, outside the limits of our well-ordered rule-of-thumb world where every effect is politely assumed to trace back to respectably explicable causes, it will scarcely be necessary to read Frazer to understand that I am not treating here of superstition. Superstition would have had naught to do with my fleeing from that mountain if word had come to my ears that these people were secretly contriving for me the black death-*ouanga*, and even fleeing I might not have been safe. White men have died in London – and the records are in Scotland Yard – because some monk in the mountains of Tibet marked them to die, and sat droning in his far-off cell among the Himalayas. A subtle poison leaving no trace? Who knows? How can one be ever sure?

But the *ouanga* packet they were now preparing to make for me was to be bright-coloured, friendly and protective, and for those very reasons I found it more difficult to view it seriously, to separate it from obvious elements which were merely superstition. Yet had I not accepted it seriously I should have been wrong, for into its making went something more than aromatic leaves and powders; into it went also the imponderable will-to-protect of a community, so that whatever it was or was not magically, it not only deserved respect but had an actual potency-value as the sacred symbol and earnest of their protection.

It was the realization of this, I think, that enabled me to see, somewhat with their eyes, as more than mummery, the ceremony of this *ouanga* packet's making.

In a small, bare room inside Maman Célie's dwelling-house, from which a sleeping-pallet and other common household gear had been removed, a large cowhide was spread, hairy side upward, on the earthern floor, and around it in a circle sat solemnly a dozen negroes whom I knew, mostly of our immediate household. There were eight men and four women. It was night time. The only light flickered upward on their faces from small candles arranged as a geometric pentagram on the cowhide. Barring the doorsill were two crossed machetes, their broad, naked blades inscribed with white chalk symbols, the swirling serpent, the phallic staff, the enmeshed triangles.

Spread in the centre of the candle pentagram, on the cowhide, was a square red cloth, like a napkin, which was to be the covering of my *ouanga* packet. Bright ribbons, red and yellow, lay beside it, and also feathers brilliantly dyed. In little, separated piles upon the cowhide were balsam leaves, leaves of the castor-bean plant, roots of the lime tree; a saucer of flour, a saucer of ashes, a bottle of *clairin*, a bottle of perfume, a tiny iron crucifix.

Maman Célie and I sat on one side in the circle, Papa Théodore facing us. While they chanted almost in undertones, '*Papa Legba, ouvri barrière pour lie; tout Mystère 'gider lie*' (Legba, open the gate for him and every Mystery protect him), old Théodore took some of the roots and leaves, mixed them in a brazier, charred them together in a mortar. The two machetes were taken from the doorsill and planted upright in the ground, flanking him on each side. A *bocor* (magician) filled his mouth with *clairin* and sprayed it, sputtering, over all the paraphernalia on the cowhide, to drive away evil spirits. While Papa Théodore continued rhythmically pounding his materials in the mortar, the *bocor* began picking up balsam leaves and castor-bean leaves, one by one, marking each with a chalked cross and depositing it on the napkin, until a new pile was made there. Atop these leaves he now laid the crucifix, also a tuft of hair (tied together with thread) which had been cut previously from the central crown of my head; a paring from my right thumb-nail, and a small square cut from a shirt which had been worn next to my skin. Something of this sort runs through all primitive magic, whether the purpose be benevolent or evil. Articles intimately connected with the individual to be affected, a part of his own body such as hair or nail-paring if it can be procured, or a piece of clothing saturated with his perspiration or grease, are used variously as a substitution for himself. One of the most dreaded forms of Haitian-African magic includes the dressing of a corpse in a garment of the person marked for vengeance and then exposing it to rot away in some secret place in the jungle. Men have gone stark mad seeking that jungle-hidden horror, and others have died hopelessly, searching. Fear, hunger, thirst, jungle-terror, one may say. Names again, tags, labels. But marked for death by the Voodoo curse, they died. In the case of the death-*ouanga* packet, poisonous leaves are used with other corroding and defiling substances. Frazer contends that for magic of this sort to operate fatally without supplementary human agency the victim must *know* and *believe*. Probably this is true. But in the case of unbelievers they sometimes make use of appallingly pragmatic methods to instil faith. I am told that when some years ago 'Bank' Williams, the saturnine, cynical, fearless Yankee manager of the bank which is Haiti's treasury, was thus marked for death, on one occasion a dog died in agony lapping pure water from the seemingly innocent clean bowl in which his morning coffee might have been poured had not the bowl been suspected, and on another occasion, deadly poison was found inside an egg whose shell had apparently never been broken. He survived, I am told, because he fought the devil with fire; for weeks, until definite events made his death no longer desired, every particle of food that passed his lips, every garment that touched his skin, first went through the hands of an old wrinkled woman from Martinique who knew every trick of black magic and served him with single-hearted fidelity.

So there was an additional element beyond anything that could be connected with credulity, superstition, or a belief in supernormal agencies that caused in me this knowledge that Voodoo magic was pragmatically effective, whether for good or evil; that caused me to believe in a definite sense that this bright, protective charm which they were engaged in preparing for me now constituted a real and actual protection. There is a queer point involved here which I find difficulty in putting into words. It will doubtless seem to many readers superstitious when I aver that I actually believe the protective virtue would have been destroyed in this charm unless I myself had faith in it. But, suppose I had sat there deeming their whole performance, well, say – silly, or funny? Suppose I had viewed it as futile, childish charlatanism? I do not mean, 'Suppose I had laughed or sneered in their faces.' I do not mean anything as clearly defined as that. These people were intuitively sensitized to shades of unexpressed feeling, almost like animals. Is it sure that if I had felt a humorous or contemptuous scorn, even secret and unexpressed, I should have been as well protected by this *ouanga*, as safe thereafter among these people in the mountain? I tell you that my believing gave it power. And connected with this truth are many deep collateral truths concerning the power of all magic, miracles, and prayer.

When Papa Théodore had finished pounding the charred aromatic herbs, the *bocor* took a pinch of the substance between his fingers and sprinkled it, muttering incantations, on the pile of green leaves surmounted by the crucifix and the objects which had been a part of myself, of my living body. All arose, and slowly circling, took similarly a pinch of the charred mixture and sprinkled it. I, last of all, was instructed to do likewise. When we were reseated, the *bocor*, with a small glowing brand from the fire, touched off successively three little piles of gunpowder on the cowhide to drive away evil spirits. Then he and Papa Théodore drew the two cabalistically marked machetes from the earth and clashed them violently together above all our heads.

Maman Célie handed me a copper coin and instructed me to place it on the packet. And now, before it was tied up, she told me to make a prayer (wish). I hesitated, then stood with both arms stretched straight out before me, palms downward, as I had seen them do and said in English:

'May Papa Legba, Maîtresse Ezilée and the Serpent protect me from misrepresenting these people, and give me power to write honestly of their mysterious religion, for all living faiths are sacred.'

On the afternoon of the Friday set for my blood baptism, more than fifty friends and relatives gathered at the habitation of Maman Célie. There was no reason to suppose that we might be disturbed, but as an extra precaution a gay *danse Congo* was immediately organized to cover the real purpose of our congregation. Maman Célie had told me that I would get no sleep that night; so despite the noise I napped until after sunset, when she awakened me and led me across the compound to the *houmfort*.

Through its outer door, which Emanuel stood guarding like a sentinel and unlocked for us, we entered a dim, windowless, cell-like anteroom in which were tethered the sacrificial beasts, a he-goat, two red cocks and two black, an enormous white turkey, and a pair of doves. Huddled there in a corner also was the girl Catherine, Maman Célie's youngest unmarried daughter; why she was there I did not know, and it is needless to say that I wondered.

From this dim, somewhat sinister antechamber we passed through an open doorway into the long, rectangular mystery room, the temple proper, which was lighted with candles and primitive oil lamps that flickered like torches. Its clay walls were elaborately painted with crude serpent symbols and anthropomorphic figures. Papa Legba, guardian of the gates, god of the crossroads, was represented as a venerable old black farmer with a pipe between his teeth; Ogoun Badagris, the bloody warrior, appeared as an old-time Haitian revolutionary general in uniform with a sword; Wangol, master of the land, drove a yoke of oxen; Agoué, master of the seas, puffed out his cheeks to blow a wind and held in the hollow of his hand a tiny boat; the serpent symbols stood for the great Damballa Oueddo, almighty Jove of the Voodoo pantheon, and his consort Ayida Oueddo.

At the near end of the room, close to the doorway through which we had entered, was the wide, low altar, spread over with a white lace tablecloth. In its centre was a small wooden serpent, elevated horizontally on a little pole as Moses lifted up the serpent in the wilderness; around this symbol, which was ancient before the Exodus, were grouped thunderstones, Christian crucifixes made in France or Germany, necklaces on which were strung snake vertebrae, others from which hung little medallions of the Virgin Mary. On the corner of the altar nearest me, my *ouanga* had been placed. Grouped also on the altar were earthern jugs containing wine, water, oil; platters of vegetables and fruits, plates containing common bread, and plates containing elaborate sweet fancy cakes, bought days before down in the plain. There were bottles of expensive French-labelled grenadine and orgeat, a bottle of rum, kola-champagne, etc. There were also three cigars, not of the rough sort the peasants smoke, but fat and smooth in their red-gilt bands. With a naïve but justifiable rationality, these worshippers, whose gods were vitally, utterly real, saw no anachronism in offering to their deities the best of everything that could be procured. Maman Célie herself, accompanied by Papa Théodore, had gone by narrow trails across mountains and valleys, leading a donkey down to the modern city, shopping there for their celestial guests and returning with the donkey's panniers heavy laden.

On the altar also was a cone-like mound of cornmeal surmounted by an egg, and before the altar candles were burning, and wicks floating in cocoanut shells of oil. At the left were the three *Rada* drums, at the right was a low wooden stool placed for me.

At the other end of the mystery room, so that a ten-foot open space was left before the altar, were seated on the ground the eighteen or twenty people, all close relatives or trusted friends, who were to witness the ceremony. When I entered, they were swaying and singing:

Papa Legba, ouvrí barrière pour moins!
Papa Legba, coté petits ou?
Papa Legba, ou oué yo!
Papa Legba, ouvrí barrière pour li passer!

(Father Legba, open wide the gate!
Father Legba, where are thy children?
Father Legba, we are here.
Father Legba, open wide the gate that he may pass!)

The *papaloi*, a powerful clean-shaven black man of middle age with red turban and a bright-coloured embroidered stole over his shoulders, traced with cornmeal a cabalistic design on the bare earth before the altar. It measured perhaps twelve feet from end to end. Its circles, it was afterwards explained to me, represented, from left to right, earth, sky, and sea. (Adepts of the esoteric will read here earth, air, and water, or if of a certain school will read earth, air, fire, and water, accepting a central sky-circle as a symbol also of the sun.) All these matters indeed entered into it, but the simpler interpretation was dominant. Forked marks, all connecting, with lines interjoining them with three circles, thence radiating towards the altar and reversely towards the worshippers, were symbols of the invisible paths through which the gods and mysteries would move.

Into the earth circle the *papaloi* poured oil, flour, and wine, while the people chanted, '*Wangol maît' la terre*' (Wangol is master of the earth). Into the sky circle he poured rum and ashes, while they chanted, '*Damballa Oueddo, ou maît' la ciel*' (Damballa Oueddo, thou art master of the sky). Into the sea circle he poured water, while they sang, '*Papa Agoué, li maît' la mer*' (Father Agoué, he is master of the sea).

A number of solos interspersed this general chanting. It was impossible to retain them all in memory. I could not make pencil notes there; not even Maman Célie was able afterwards to repeat them all for me, and the next day some of the singers were gone. There was one song to Papa Agoué, however, which I partly remembered because it had seemed to me beautiful, and later I rode to find the singer and transcribe it. It was:

Agoué, woyó! woyó!
Maîtr' Agoué reter lans la mer;
Li tirer canot.

Bassin blé
Reter toi zilet;

Nèg coqui' lans mer zorage;
Li tirer canot là.

Agoué, woyó! woyó!

(Hail to Father Agoué
Who dwells in the sea!
He is the Lord of ships.

In the blue gulf
There are three little islands.
The negro's boat is storm-tossed,
Father Agoué brings it safely in.
Hail to Father Agoué!)

When this singing and pouring of libations were ended, the *papaloi* sealed the open doorway by tracing across its earthen sill. Evil or unwelcome forces which sought to enter would become entangled in the lines and go wandering from circle to circle like lost souls among the stars.

This done, he began the real service, for which all thus far had been but a preparation. He stood with arms raised before the altar and said solemnly, '*Lans nom tout Loi et tout Mystère*' (In the name of all the Gods and all the Mysteries).

Maman Célie advanced at a sign from the *papaloi* and was invested by him, with the scarlet robe and headdress of ostrich feathers black and red, as *mamaloi* or priestess. This was accompanied by a shrill chant:

Ayida Oueddo, ou couleuvre moins!
Qui lé ou filer ou cou z'éclai!

(Ayida Oueddo, my serpent goddess,
When you come it is like the lightning flash!)

At the same time now I heard through the chanting a sharp long-drawn continuous hissing. It was Maman

Célie, hissing like a snake, drawing and expelling the breath through her teeth.

I looked for Maman Célie's familiar sweet, gentle face, but beneath the black and scarlet plumes I saw now only what seemed a rigid mask. I felt that I was looking into the face of a strange, dreadful woman, or into the face of something which I had never seen before. As I watched, the cheeks of this black mask were deeply indrawn so that the face became skull-like, and then alternately puffed out as if the skull had been covered with flesh and come alive.

As the chanting died away, she whirled three times and flung herself prostrate before the altar with her lips pressed against the earth.

Emanuel, without donning sacerdotal garb, but now acting as a sort of altar servant, brought in the two red cocks. Each was handled gently, almost reverently, by the *papaloi*, as he knelt holding it and with white flour traced on its back a cross. One of the small sweet cakes was crumbled, and each cock must peck at it from the *mamaloi's* hand. This was awaited patiently. At the moment when each bird consented to receive the consecrated food, the priestess seized it and rose wildly dancing, whirling with the cock held by its head and feet in her upstretched hands, its wings violently fluttering. Round and round she whirled while the drums throbbed in a quick, tangled, yet steady rhythm. With a sudden twist the cock's head was torn off and as she whirled the blood flew out as if from a sprinkling-pot. The other birds, the black cocks and the doves, were dealt with similarly. As she danced with the white living doves, it was beautiful, and it seemed to me natural also that they should presently die. Blood of the doves was saved in a china cup.

A thing which had a different, a horror-beauty like a mad Goya etching, occurred when the black priestess did her death dance with the huge white turkey. Though far from feeble, possessed of great vitality, she was a slender woman, slightly formed, whose nervous strength lay not in muscular weight. When the turkey's wings spread wide and began to flap frantically above her head as she whirled, the great bird seemed larger and more powerful than she; it seemed that she would be dragged from her feet, hurled to the ground, or flown away with fabulously into the sky. And as she sought finally to tear off its head, sought to clutch its body between her knees, it attacked her savagely, beating her face and breasts, beating at her so that she was at moments enfolded by the great white wings, so that bird and woman seemed to mingle struggling in a monstrous, mythical embrace. But her fatal hands were still upon its throat, and in that swanlike simulacre of the deed which for the male is always like a little death, it died.

So savage had this scene been that it was almost like an anti-climax when the sacrificial goat was now led through the doorway to the altar, but new and stranger things, contrasting, were yet to happen before other blood was shed. He was a sturdy brown young goat, with big, blue, terrified, almost human eyes, eyes which seemed not only terrified but aware and wondering. At first he bleated and struggled, for the odour of death was in the air, but finally he stood quiet, though still wide-eyed, while red silken ribbons were twined in his little horns, his little hoofs anointed with wine and sweet-scented oils, and an old woman who had come from far over the mountain for this her one brief part in the long ceremony sat down before him and crooned to him alone a song which might have been a baby's lullaby.

When it was finished, the *papaloi* sat down before the little goat and addressed to it a discourse in earnest tones. He told the little goat that it would soon pass through the final gates before us all, instructed it in the mysteries, and pleaded with it concerning its conduct on the other side. But before it passed through the gate, he explained, certain magical changes, making its path easier, would occur on this side. Therefore it need have no fear. Upon its forehead he traced a cross and circle, first with flour and afterwards with blood of the doves. Then he presented to it a green, leafy branch to eat.

This goat had by now become inevitably personal to me. I had conceived an affectionate interest in him while the old woman was singing. I recalled what had happened to the other creatures at the moment they touched food, and I had an impulse to cry out to him, 'Don't do that, little goat! Don't touch it!' But it was a fleeting, purely sentimental impulse. Not for anything, no matter what would happen, could I have seriously wished to stop that ceremony. I believe in such ceremonies. I hope that they will never die out or be abolished. I believe that in some form or another they answer a deep need of the universal human soul. I, who in a sense believe in no religion, believe yet in them all, asking only that they be alive – as religions. Codes of rational ethics and human brotherly love are useful, but they do not touch this thing underneath. Let religion have its bloody sacrifices, yes, even human sacrifices, if thus our souls may be kept alive. Better a black *papaloi* in Haiti with blood-stained hands who believes in his living gods than a frock-coated minister on Fifth Avenue reducing Christ to a solar myth and rationalizing the Immaculate Conception.

And so I did not cry out.

And the goat nibbled the green leaves.

But no knife flashed.

In the dim, bare anteroom with its windowless grey walls, the girl Catherine had remained all this time huddled in a corner, as if drugged or half asleep.

Emanuel had to clutch her tightly by the arm to

prevent her from stumbling when they brought her to the altar. Maman Célie hugged her and moaned and shed tears as if they were saying good-bye forever. The *papaloi* pulled them apart, and someone gave the girl a drink of rum from a bottle. She began to protest in a dull sort of angry, whining way when they forced her down on her knees before the lighted candles. The *papaloi* wound round her forehead red ribbons like those which had been fastened around the horns of the goat, and Maman Célie, no longer as a mourning mother but as an officiating priestess, with rigid face aided in pouring the oil and wine on the girl's head, feet, hands, and breast.

All this time the girl had been like a fretful, sleepy, annoyed child, but gradually she became docile, sombre, staring with quiet eyes, and presently began a weird song of lamentation. I think she was extemporizing both the words and the melody. She sang:

Cochon marron saché chemin caille;
Moins mandé ça li gagnin.
'Nans Léogane tout moon malade O!'

Béf marron saché chemin caille.
Moins mandé ça li gagnin.
'Nans gros morne tout moon malade O!'

Cabrit marron saché chemin caille.
Moins mandé ça li gagnin.
'Nans Guinea tout moon malade O!'

M'pas malade, m'a p'mourri!
(The wild pig came seeking me;
I said why have you come?
'Every one is sick in Léogane!'

The wild bull came seeking me;
I said why have you come?
'Every one is sick in the mountains!'

The wild goat came seeking me;
I said why have you come?
'Every one is sick in Africa!'

So I who am not sick must die!)

And so that black girl sang, and as the inner meaning of her song came to me, I seemed to hear the voice of Jephtha's daughter doomed to die by her own father as a sacrifice to Javeh, going up to bewail her virginity on Israel's lonely mountain. Her plight in actuality was rather that of Isaac bound by Abraham on Mount Moriah; a horned beast would presently be substituted in her stead; but the moment for that mystical substitution had not yet come, and as she sang she was a daugher doomed to die.

The ceremony of substitution, when it came, was pure effective magic of a potency which I have never seen equalled in Dervish monastery or anywhere. The goat and the girl, side by side before the altar, had been startled, restive, nervous. The smell of blood was in the air, but there was more than that hovering; it was the eternal, mysterious odour of death itself which both animals and human beings always sense, but not through the nostrils. Yet now the two who were about to die mysteriously merged, the girl symbolically and the beast with a knife in its throat, were docile and entranced, were like automatons. The *papaloi* monotonously chanting, endlessly repeating, 'Damballa calls you, Damballa calls you,' stood facing the altar with arms outstretched above their two heads. The girl was now on her hands and knees in the attitude of a quadruped, directly facing the goat, so that their heads and eyes were on a level, less than ten inches apart, and thus they stared fixedly into each other's eyes, while the *papaloi's* hands weaved slowly, ceaselessly above their foreheads, the forehead of the girl and the forehead of the horned beast, each wound with red ribbons, each already marked with the blood of a white dove. By shifting slightly I could see the big, wide, pale-blue, staring eyes of the goat, and the big, black, staring eyes of the girl, and I could have almost sworn that the black eyes were gradually, mysteriously becoming those of a dumb beast, while a human soul was beginning to peer out through the blue. But dismiss that, and still I tell you that pure magic was here at work, that something very real and fearful was occurring. For as the priest wove his ceaseless incantations, the girl began a low, piteous bleating in which there was nothing, absolutely nothing, human; and soon a thing infinitely more unnatural occurred; the goat was moaning and crying like a human child. I believe that through my Druse and Yezidee accounts I have earned a deserved reputation for being not too credulous in the face of marvels. But I was in the presence now of a thing that could not be denied. Old magic was here at work, and it worked appallingly. What difference does it make whether we call it supernatural or merely supernormal? What difference does it make if we say that the girl was drugged – as I suspect she was – or that both were hypnotized? Of course they were, if you like. And what then? We live surrounded by mysteries and imagine that by inventing names we explain them.

Other signs and wonders became manifest. Into this little temple lost among the mountains came in answer to goat-cry girl-cry the Shaggy Immortal One of a thousand names whom the Greeks called Pan. The goat's lingam became erect and rigid, the points of the girl's breasts visibly hardened and were outlined sharply pressing against the coarse, thin, tight-drawn shift that was her only garment. Thus they faced each other motionless as two marble figures on the frieze of some ancient phallic temple. They were like inanimate twin lamps in which a sacred flame burned, steadily yet unconsuming.

While the *papaloi* still wove his spells, his hands

moving ceaselessly like an old woman carding wool in a dream, the priestess held a twig green with tender leaves between the young girl and the animal. She held it on a level with their mouths, and neither saw it, for they were staring fixedly into each other's eyes as entranced mediums stare into crystal globes, and with their necks thrust forward so that their foreheads almost touched. Neither could therefore see the leafy branch, but as the old *mamaloi's* hand trembled, the leaves flicked lightly as if stirred by a little breeze against the hairy muzzle of the goat, against the chin and soft lips of the girl. And after moments of breathless watching, it was the girl's lips which pursed out and began to nibble at the leaves. Human beings, normally, when eating, open their mouths and take the food directly in between their teeth. Except for sipping liquids they do not use their lips. But the girl's lips now nibbling at the leaves were like those of a ruminating animal. Her hands, of course, were flat on the ground so that in a sense she perforce must have eaten without using them, somewhat in the manner of a quadruped; but in a castle near the edge of the Nefud desert I once watched closely a woman eating whose hands were tied behind her back, and that woman, opening her mouth and baring her teeth, took the fragments of food directly between her teeth, as any normal human being would. But this girl now pursed her lips and used them nibbling as horned cattle do. It sounds a slight thing, perhaps, in the describing, but it was weird, unnatural, unhuman.

As she nibbled thus, the *papaloi* said in a hushed but wholly matter-of-fact whisper like a man who had finished a hard, solemn task and was glad to rest, '*Ca y est*' (There it is).

The *papaloi* was now holding a machete, ground sharp and shining. Maman Célie, priestess, kneeling, held a *gamelle*, a wooden bowl. It was oblong. There was just space enough to thrust it narrowly between the mystically identified pair. Its rim touched the goat's hairy chest and the girl's body, both their heads thrust forward above it. Neither seemed conscious of anything that was occurring, nor did the goat flinch when the *papaloi* laid his hand upon its horns. Nor did the goat utter any sound as the knife was drawn quickly, deeply across its throat. But at this instant, as the blood gushed like a fountain into the wooden bowl, the girl, with a shrill, piercing, then strangled bleat of agony, leaped, shuddered, and fell senseless before the altar.

At the moment the knife flashed across the goat's throat, the company had begun to chant, not high or loud but with a sort of deep, hushed fervour, across which the girl's inhuman bleating had shrilled sharp as another invisible blade. Now they continued chanting while the celebrants performed their various offices. They chanted:

Damballa Oueddo odan q'icit
Mandé ça la! Oué!
Ayida Oueddo odan q'icit
Mandé ça la! Oué!

(Damballa and Ayida, behold the deed we have done as you commanded).

The body of the goat was thrown as a ritually useless and no longer sacred thing through the door into the anteroom. The body of the unconscious girl, spattered with blood, was lifted carefully into Emanuel's arms and carried away, followed by two old women versed in magic who would attend her recovery. If Maman Célie, her face still like a terrible, inspired mask, bestowed one fleeting glance on either body, I did not see it. She was revolving slowly before the altar with the bowl in her outstretched arms and now held it to the *papaloi*, who received it, drank, then placed it on the altar, and with a little china cup poured libations within each of the three cabalistic circles on the earth. They also sang an invocation to Ybo, another of the ancient gods.

There was a pause, a lull, in which I who had been for hours too utterly absorbed to give myself a thought, recalled that all this ceremonial was leading up to an event which concerned me more deeply than any other present. The time had now come. A very old black man, deeply wrinkled, with a beard that was like Spanish moss turned snowy white, who had been sitting silent all the while, took from a bag at his feet a white cloth which he wound around his head, and a white embroidered garment like a cassock which he put over his shoulders. He invested himself without the aid of other hands as a black pope or emperor might have done. He was not of our mountain. He had come riding upon a donkey from beyond the great Morne. Maman Célie had summoned him and had paid the expenses from her own purse. It was a thing for which she would never permit me to repay her. As he arose and beckoned me to kneel at last before the altar, there was absolute silence. He was Voodoo of the Voodoo, but as he laid his hand upon my head it was neither in Creole that he spoke, nor French, nor even the almost forgotten language of old Guinea. I heard as in a dream, low, clear, and deep as the voices of old men rarely are, '*In nomine Patris, et Filii, et Spiritus Sancti. Amen.*'

And when still kneeling there with my eyes closed, I heard as from a great distance and as an echo from years long past his sure voice intoning that most marvellous and mysterious of all Latin invocations, 'Rosa Mystica . . . Tower of David . . . Tower of Ivory . . . House of Gold . . . Gate of Heaven,' it seemed to me that I heard too the rolling of mighty organs beneath vaulted domes . . .

Oil, wine, and water were poured upon my head, marks were traced upon my brow with white flour, and then I was given to eat ritually from the cakes upon the altar, to drink from the wine, rum, and syrups there. Parts of many cakes were crumbled together in a little cup and were put into my mouth with a spoon; likewise were mingled a few drops from each of the many bottles.

This, it seemed, had been a preliminary consecration rite in sincere inclusion of the Christian divinities, saints, and powers. Now the Voodoo chanting recommenced, and for the first time my own name was mingled with the Creole and African words. They were beseeching Legba to open wide the gates for me, Damballa and Ayida to receive me. A sort of mad fervour was again taking possession of them all. The old *hougan*, shouting now so that his voice could be heard above the singing, demanded once more silence, and placing both hands heavily upon my head, pronounced a long mixed African and Creole invocation, calling down to witness all the gods and goddesses of ancient Africa. Still commanding silence, he dipped his hand into the wooden bowl and traced on my forehead the bloody Voodoo cross.

Then he lifted the bowl, hesitated for a queer instant as if in courteous doubt – it was a strange, trivial thing to occur at such a moment – and then picked up a clean spoon. Maman Célie interfered angrily. So the bowl itself was held to my lips and three times I drank. The blood had a clean, warm, salty taste. In physical fact, I was drinking the blood of a recently slain goat, but by some mysterious transubstantiation not without its parallels in more than one religion other than Voodoo, I was drinking the blood of the girl Catherine who in the body of the goat had mystically died for me and for all miserable humanity from Léogane to Guinea.

One small thing yet remained to be done. I had been told that it would be done, and its meaning explained to me. I had been told also that for no white man alive or dead had it ever been done before. The *papaloi* took from the altar an egg which had surmounted a little pyramid of cornmeal, and holding it aloft in his cupped hands, pronounced incantation. As the blood had represented the mystery of death, sacrifice, and purification, likewise fertilization as it was poured upon the earth, the egg now represented rebirth, productivity, fertility, re-creation. Maman Célie, the priestess, took it from the hands of the *papaloi*, traced with it a new cross on my forehead, and dashed it to the earth. My knees were spattered. Then the priestess tore off her feathered headdress, and Maman Célie, the old woman, sank down beside me, put her arms around me, and cried, 'Legba, Papa Legba, open wide the gates for this my little one.'

Green Jewel of Death

Princess Catherine Radziwill

To say that one emerald – no matter how huge – affected the history of a great nation for more than three hundred years is to create at once what lawyers call a reasonable doubt. And to suggest further that its influence was due to an ancient curse put upon the stone is not only a sure way to win ridicule, but also to be accused of an imagination lacking originality.

So let me say at the outset that I do not believe the legend about the Great Emerald being bewitched.

After one has come to America and has become a citizen of a nation with a rational history, and when one rides in subways and works in tall steel buildings, one forgets such things. Yet I must admit that when I first saw the green light of that big stone glittering from the bosom of the Empress Alexandra, and heard the indiscreet whisper of the story from a lady of the court as she counted off on her fingers the Great Emerald's victims, I was inclined to be credulous. For all of the story, except the part about the witch, is plain history that anyone may read.

There *was* such a man as Nikita Romanoff, and there *was* such a man as Boulouk Khan with a beautiful daughter. Nikita Romanoff *did* die a horrible death, and many Romanoffs thereafter, with the jewel always at hand to reflect tragedies in its cold green facets.

Remember, the last Czar and the Empress Alexandra were murdered in that cellar at Ekaterinburg *after* I had heard the story! So, you see, it is not an easy story to forget. Let me tell it as simply as possible.

First, a necessary bit of political history. When Ivan the Terrible died in 1584, he left the throne to his son, the feeble-minded Feodor. Then followed the 'troubled years' of Russian history, when Tartars, Poles, and Swedes fought for possession of Russia's dreary and lonesome plains and for the conquest of the three hundred churches and shrines of stately Moscow, with the great treasures they contained.

Fortunately, perhaps, for Russia, Feodor was married to a beautiful woman, Irene Godounoff, who contrived that her famous brother, Boris, should rule the land in Feodor's name. This Boris Godounoff was a determined, relentless man, full of ambition, who made up his mind to become the next Czar. So when Feodor died, and Irene was hailed as Czarina by the assembled nobles, or boyars, as they were called, she refused the throne, and with her own hands placed on her brother's head the crown her husband had worn.

Boris triumphed, yet he knew himself to be a usurper. He knew that, even after Feodor's younger brother, Dmitry, had been assassinated at his command, there still existed lawful successors to the Russian throne in the persons of the Romanoffs, direct descendants of the great Rurik.

There were three of these Romanoffs – Feodor, Ivan, and Nikita – and to their destruction Boris set his hand.

The first was forced to enter holy orders after having been separated from his wife, Marfa, who was shut up in the solitude of the Ipatieff Convent in Kostroma. (What Boris never knew was that, thanks to the connivance of the Abbess of Ipatieff, Marfa continued to see her husband, and gave birth to a son who was one day to become the first of the Romanoff czars.)

The second brother, Ivan, died of a mysterious illness with which was mixed up a suspicion of poison. But the third, Nikita, was not so easy to dispose of. He had too many friends.

He was handsome and brave, beloved by women and popular with men. He was truly a hero of romance, and romantic adventures followed him throughout his career.

Nikita was the only one of the Romanoffs who did not care for politics, and who had no ambition to see the diadem of the Monomaques put upon his head. He cared only for a good time, to look into the dark eyes of a lovely maiden, or to enjoy a sumptuous banquet. He, the pious orthodox descendant of that Grand Duchess Olga who had brought Christianity to Russia, had become infatuated with an infidel, with a Moslem girl, the only daughter of a Tartar Prince, Boulouk Khan.

Boulouk – one of the few Tartars whose family had remained in Moscow after the khans had been driven back to Kazan – lived very quietly in a small house under the very ramparts of the Kremlin, and received few people. One of them, however, was Nikita Romanoff.

Nikita had met the beautiful Isma by chance, at a banquet given by the Czarina; and although Moslem women were not allowed to show their faces to men, he contrived to have an affair with her, and out of it a son was born.

Boulouk Khan asked Nikita to marry the girl. The younger boyar refused, saying that his religion forbade him to unite himself in wedlock with an infidel. The tartar was furious, but kept silent.

So far, we have nothing but historical facts. Now

comes the legend, which I will relate in the form that has come down to this day. It seems that Boulouk Khan, on the night following his interview with Nikita, went to seek the help of an old and famous witch.

The old woman received him in her den, a dark, underground cavern in a lonesome spot shunned by everybody. She listened to Boulouk's story and then asked him:

'You wish to be revenged on this man for the wrong he has done your daughter?'

'Yes, I do,' replied the Tartar, 'and not only on him but on all his race in the centuries to come.'

The hag laughed, a harsh and cruel laugh.

'Your wish will be granted,' she said, 'and your revenge will perhaps be more terrible than you suspect. Wait a moment!'

She retired behind a curtain that divided her gruesome abode, and after a few minutes returned, holding in her hand an uncut emerald set in gold, fashioned as a clasp for a man's cloak.

The Tartar extended his hand towards it.

'Don't touch it!' exclaimed the old woman. 'Don't touch it until I allow you to. The devil himself is in that stone.'

She walked towards a cauldron and dipped the jewel in it, murmuring as she did so strange words in a strange language. Then she came back to where the terrified Boulouk Khan was standing.

'Here,' she said, 'take the jewel. Its beauty is unsurpassed, and its worth will go on increasing as the years pass by. But it is an accursed stone, and it will bring misfortune, sorrow, suffering, and death to all those who will possess it. Give it to Nikita Romanoff and you will see what havoc it will work. Now leave me the purse I see hanging from your waist, and go away from here, for this is no place for any but the Master of Evil to loiter in!'

That is the legend of the origin of the Great Emerald. Now we turn back to history, and find Boulouk Khan writing the following letter to Nikita Romanoff, the text of which has been preserved in the Russian archives:

Boulouk Khan, the humble servant of the great and mighty Boyar Nikita Nikitich Romanoff, humbly craves his presence at a banquet at his house, and hopes he will honour his slave with his presence at it.

'The old dog evidently has forgotten all about his anger of the other day, and wants to make amends for it,' the young man must have thought.

He went to the feast and enjoyed himself immensely.

Boulouk Khan had spared neither money nor trouble to make it sumptuous, and the day was already dawning before anyone thought of retiring. As Nikita was preparing to depart, his host stopped him.

'Great and mighty Boyar,' he said, 'grant me one last favour before you leave my house. Here is a stone that came to me from my ancestors, and which is supposed to have belonged to our great Genghis Khan himself. I have had it set as a clasp for your cloak. Honour me by accepting it, just to prove to me that you bear me no ill will for any differences we may have had in the past.'

With these words he handed over to the astonished young man the Great Emerald.

Three nights later Nikita Romanoff was sound asleep in the arms of a woman to whom, it is said, he had been secretly married, when a great noise at the door of his room awakened him. The house was surrounded and invaded by a troop of armed men, the soldiers of Boris Godounoff.

Whether the usurper, who had spies everywhere, had heard the tale of the Great Emerald and fancied that the powers of darkness were now on his side, or whether he had simply become weary of waiting and decided to risk the anger of Nikita's friends, we shall never know. The fact remains that the young Boyar was seized and bound with heavy chains and thrown into a sledge waiting at his door.

He protested and cried out for help; but all his servants had been put out of the way, and, in spite of the entreaties of his wife, he was hurried away. For long weeks the prisoner and his guards travelled towards the Siberian wastes, Nikita lying on his back at the bottom of the sledge, so tightly chained he could move neither hand nor foot. All his money had been taken away; but, by design or coincidence, the emerald of Boulouk Khan had been left in his possession.

At last the sledge stopped in the midst of an apparently endless plain. Night was beginning to fall.

The officer in command of the escort gave a brisk order, and two men began digging a hole in the frozen ground. When the men climbed out of the deep pit they had made, the officer measured the depth of it and nodded his head.

He gave a signal, and the soldiers seized Nikita and flung him into the deep hole. The top was covered over with a rude roof and without further ado the escort rode away.

Nikita Romanoff lived on for three long years, sunk in the pit, without even the possibility of looking up at the sky. From time to time a piece of bread was thrown down and a pitcher of water lowered to him. At last, one day, the guard, hearing no sound from the living tomb, peered down and saw that Nikita Romanoff was dead at last.

They did not remove his body. Godounoff had given his orders, and all that was done was to fill up the pit with earth.

Time went on, and after Godounoff's death Nikita's nephew, Michael Romanoff, was hailed as Czar by the Muscovite boyars in the Ipatieff Convent at Kostroma. The new dynasty began its reign, which was to last exactly three hundred and four years.

Nikita Romanoff lay in his unconsecrated grave, forgotten by the world, until the day when, for a short period, Russia was ruled by a woman – the handsome, imperious Czarina Sophia, sister of the man who was to be known as Peter the Great.

She remembered the dark story of the victim of Godounoff's ambition and cruelty and sent men to Siberia with instructions to look for the mortal remains of her murdered kinsman. When they were found, she had them properly buried, and a chapel erected on the spot of his awful martyrdom.

Among the remnants of clothes dug from Nikita Romanoff's grave was found the Great Emerald of Boulouk Khan. Its gold setting had not tarnished, and the jewel itself had lost none of its weird beauty. The Czarina's messengers brought it back to her, and Sophia found it so fascinating that she immediately began to wear it on a chain around her neck. Her attendants and even her confessor warned her against it, for by this time the legend of the curse was being whispered around Moscow.

Sophia laughed at these warnings. She believed herself absolutely secure.

But the boy under whose name she was reigning was the great Peter. He also wanted to reign, and to reign alone.

One day Sophia was rudely dragged out of her Kremlin Palace and thrust into a convent. Only once did she ever emerge from her cell. This was on a fateful afternoon when, by order of her brother, she was taken to a window under which a scaffold had been erected and was forced to see each one of her faithful Stryeltsi officers led up in succession and beheaded. The miserable woman fainted at last, and, when she recovered her senses, found herself back in her religious prison, where she remained until her death.

But, before she had been led away from the Terem she was never to see again, the Czarina had contrived to squeeze into the hand of Eudoxia Lopoukhina, the wife of her brother Peter, the emerald of Nikita Romanoff. Not long afterwards, Eudoxia also fell into disgrace, and was banished by her merciless husband to make way for the Livonian peasant girl who was to become Empress of All the Russias.

When Eudoxia was bidding goodbye to her only son, Alexis, she gave him the emerald.

This unbalanced youth, who imagined himself strong enough to resist the will of his father, the Great White Czar, was tortured to death in the dark dungeons of the fortress of Saints Peter and Paul. Peter himself lashed him with the knout, and dealt the blow that killed him.

Alexis turned his eyes upon the Czar, and murmured, 'Father, I forgive you!' then feebly put his hands to a little silk bag he wore around his neck, and clung to it until death mercifully released him. In the bag was Nikita Romanoff's emerald. It was brought to Peter after his son's body had been laid in his coffin. But the Emperor refused to touch it; instead he had it taken to the Treasury and put under lock and key.

There it remained until his niece, the Empress Anna Ivanovna, ascended the throne of Russia. The first time she looked through the imperial jewels, she took a fancy to the stone and presented it to her favourite, the famous Biren, who became Duke of Courland. The latter was disgraced and sent into exile by Anna's successor, the Empress Elizabeth Petrovna.

Remembering the evil reputation the stone possessed, Biren sent it back to his sovereign, in the hope, it was said, that it would work her evil. Elizabeth, however, did not care for it. She had it set in a ring, which she gave to her nephew – the man who later became Peter III.

Peter was celebrating his marriage to a young girl who later became known as Catherine the Great. Those who doubt the Great Emerald's evil influence point out that the sole gift of Catherine's hand would have been enough to bring tragedy into any man's life – even a nobler one than the coarse and brutal Peter.

The fact remains, though that not long after Peter succeeded his aunt to the throne, he was deposed by the Palace Guards and later strangled in the castle of Ropscha by Gregory Orloff, Catherine's favourite.

The emerald of Nikita Romanoff was removed from his finger with great difficulty after his death and brought back to the Imperial Treasury. The Empress Catherine refused at first to have anything to do with it.

The great sovereign was not a superstitious woman, yet somehow this stone inspired terror in her.

One day, after many years had passed and the murder that had taken place at Ropscha was beginning to be forgotten, curiosity overcame her. She had the Great Emerald brought to her, and was so captivated with its beauty that she decided to have it reset as an ornament for Marie Feodorovna, the wife of her son Paul. Two hours after she had sent for the court jeweller to discuss the matter with him, Catherine was struck down by an apoplectic fit and died that same evening.

After this, no one at court would touch without gloves the emerald of Nikita Romanoff, and friends urged Paul I to get rid of it. But the Emperor refused to entertain the idea of parting with this remarkable jewel. Instead, he had it set in the handle of a sword to wear on state occasions.

On the evening of the day when Paul had worn the sword for the first time, conspirators, acting under the direction of his son Alexander, broke into the Czar's bed-chamber, demanding his abdication.

Paul leaped up and seized the sword that bore the Great Emerald and attempted to defend himself. In the scuffle the stone was broken from its setting – and its owner mortally wounded.

Paul's son, Alexander I, would never even look at the jewel, and conceived the idea of presenting it to some church or shrine. But his confessor, the famous Abbot Photius, told him this could not be done, because the stone was supposed to have been cursed by Satan himself. This opinion the next sovereign, Nicholas I, seemed to share, and as long as he occupied the throne Nikita Romanoff's emerald remained hidden away in one of the strong-boxes of the Imperial Treasury.

There it lay until, many years later, the morganatic wife of Alexander II, the Princess Dolgorouky, having heard its sinister story, asked her husband to allow her to examine it. The Czar himself had never seen the fateful emerald, and when it was brought to him one morning at breakfast, he admired it immensely – so much, indeed, that, after having promised his consort to have it set for her in a pendant, he put it in his pocket to show to his favourite cousin, the Grand Duchess Catherine Michaelovna, with whom he was to dine that day.

On his way back to the Winter Palace, Alexander was blown to pieces by bombs thrown at him by nihilist conspirators.

The next day a police officer picked the emerald out of a snow bank on the spot where the Czar had fallen, and took it to the palace.

Once again Nikita Romanoff's jewel went into retirement. Alexander III and his consort, the Empress Marie, believed absolutely in its uncanny influence, and would not even allow it to be kept in any of the strong-boxes where their personal belongings were stored. The Empress, in particular, never wished it to be even mentioned in her presence, and is to this day persuaded that it caused all the calamities of the Romanoff dynasty.

Perhaps it was out of opposition to the Empress Marie that her daughter-in-law, the late Alexandra, refused to admit that a mere jewel could bring misfortune. She persuaded Czar Nicholas II to have the emerald set into a pendant, which she wore continually.

It was on Alexandra's neck that I saw this fatal jewel.

She took it with her into exile when she went with her husband and her children to Siberia. Doubtless she was wearing it on that fatal and mysterious night in Ekaterinburg when the great Romanoff dynasty came to its tragic end.

Where is Nikita Romanoff's emerald now?

No one seems to know.

It has not appeared among the crown jewels that have been sold by the present rulers of Russia.

Superstitious people may be tempted to say that, having worked out its curse, it has been taken back by the devil to whom it belonged. But that, of course, is nonsense.

The Phantom Coach

Elma B. Edwards

The circumstances I am about to relate to you have truth to commend them. They happened to me, and my recollection of them is as vivid as if they had taken place only yesterday. Twenty years, however, have gone by since that night. During those twenty years I have told the story to but one other person. I tell it now with a reluctance which I find it difficult to overcome. All I ask, meanwhile, is that you will abstain from forcing your own conclusions upon me. I want nothing explained away. I desire no arguments. My mind on this subject is quite made up, and, having the testimony of my own senses to rely upon, I prefer to abide by it.

Well! It was just twenty years ago, and within a day or two of the end of the grouse season. I had been out all day with my gun, and had had no sport to speak of. The wind was due east; the month, December; the place, a bleak wide moor in the far north of England. And I had lost all sense of direction. It was not a pleasant place in which to lose one's way, with the first feathery flakes of a coming snowstorm just fluttering down upon the heather, and the leaden evening closing in all around. I shaded my eyes with my hand, and stared anxiously into the gathering darkness, where the purple moorland melted into a range of low hills, some ten or twelve miles distant. Not the faintest smoke-wreath, not the tiniest cultivated patch, or fence, or sheep-track, met my eyes in any direction. There was nothing for it but to walk on, and take my chance of finding what shelter I could, by the way. So I shouldered my gun again and pushed wearily forward, for I had been on foot since an hour after daybreak and had eaten nothing since breakfast.

Meanwhile, the snow began to come down with ominous persistence, and the wind fell. After this, the cold became more intense, and the night came rapidly on. As for me, my prospects worsened with the darkening sky, and my heart grew heavy as I thought how my young wife was already watching for me through the window of our little inn parlour, and thought of all the suffering in store for her throughout this weary night. We had been married four months, and, having spent our autumn in the Highlands, were now lodging in a remote little village situated just on the verge of the great English moorlands. We were very much in love, and, of course, very happy. This morning, when we parted, she had implored me to return before dusk, and I had promised her that I would. What would I not have given to have kept my word!

Even now, weary as I was, I felt that with a supper, an hour's rest, and a guide, I might still get back to her before midnight, if only some help could be found.

And all this time the snow fell and the night became darker. I stopped and shouted every now and then, but my cries seemed only to emphasize the silence that reigned everywhere. Then a vague sense of uneasiness came upon me, and I began to remember stories of travellers who had walked on and on in the falling snow until, exhausted, they sank down to embrace a sleep from which they never awoke. Would it be possible, I asked myself, to keep going all through the long, lonely night? Would there not come a time when my limbs must fail, and my resolution give way? When I, too, must sleep the sleep of death. Death! I shuddered. How hard to die just now, when life a few hours ago had seemed so full of promise! How hard for my darling, whose loving heart – but that thought was not to be borne! To banish it, I shouted again, louder and longer, and then listened eagerly. Was my shout answered, or did I only fancy that I heard a far-off cry? I halloed again, and again the echo followed. Then a wavering speck of light came suddenly out of the dark, shifting, disappearing, growing momentarily nearer and brighter. Running towards it as quickly as I could, I found myself, to my great joy, face to face with an old man and a lantern.

'Thank God!' was the exclamation that burst involuntarily from my lips.

Blinking and frowning, he lifted his lantern and peered into my face.

'What for?' growled he, sulkily.

'Well – for you. I began to fear I should be lost in the snow.'

'Eh, then, folks do get cast away hereabouts fra', time to time, an' what's to hinder you from bein' cast away likewise, if the Lord's so minded?'

'If the Lord is so minded that you and I shall be lost together, friend, we must submit,' I replied; 'but I don't mean to be lost without you. How far am I now from Dwolding?'

'A gude twenty mile, more or less.'

'And the nearest village?'

'The nearest village is Wyke, an' that's twelve mile 'other side.'

'Where do you live, then?'

'Out yonder,' said he, with a vague jerk of the lantern.

'You're going home, I presume?'

'Maybe I am.'

'Then I'm going with you.'

The old man shook his head, and rubbed his nose reflectively with the handle of the lantern.

'It ain't o' no use,' growled he. 'He won't let you in – not he.'

'We'll see about that,' I replied, briskly. 'Who is He?'

'The master.'

'Who is the master?'

'That's nowt to you,' was the unceremonious reply.

'Well, well; you lead the way, and I'll see to it that the master shall give me shelter and a supper tonight.'

'Eh, you can try him!' muttered my reluctant guide; and, still shaking his head, he hobbled, gnome-like, away through the falling snow. A large mass loomed up presently out of the darkness, and a huge dog rushed out, barking furiously.

'Is this the house?' I asked.

'Ay, it's the house. Down, Bey!' And he fumbled in his pocket for the key.

I drew up immediately behind him, determined to go in with him, and saw in the little circle of light shed by the lantern that the door was heavily studded with iron nails, like that of a prison. In another minute he had turned the key and I had pushed past him into the house.

Once inside, I looked round with curiosity, and found myself in a great raftered hall, which served, apparently, a variety of uses. One end was piled to the roof with corn, like a barn. The other was stored with flour-sacks, agricultural implements, casks, and all kinds of miscellaneous lumber; while from the beams overhead hung rows of hams, flitches, and bunches of dried herbs for winter use. In the centre of the floor stood a large object gauntly dressed in a dingy wrapping-cloth, and reaching half way to the rafters. Lifting a corner of this cloth, I saw, to my surprise, a telescope of considerable size, mounted on a rough moveable platform, with four small wheels. The tube was made of painted wood, bound round with bands of metal; the speculum, so far as I could estimate its size in the dim light, measured at least fifteen inches in diameter. While I was yet examining the instrument, and asking myself whether it was not the work of some self-taught star-gazer, a bell rang sharply.

'That's for you,' said my guide, with a malicious grin. 'Yonder's his room.'

He pointed to a low black door at the opposite side of the hall. I crossed over, rapped somewhat loudly, and went in, without waiting for an invitation. A huge, white-haired old man rose from a table covered with books and papers, and confronted me sternly.

'Who are you?' said he. 'How came you here? What do you want?'

'James Murray, barrister-at-law. On foot across the moor. Meat, drink, and sleep.'

He bent his bushy brows into a portentous frown.

'Mine is not a house of entertainment,' he said, haughtily. 'Jacob, how dare you admit this stranger?'

'I didn't admit him,' grumbled the old man. 'He followed me over the muir, and shouldered his way in before me. I'm no match for six foot two.'

'Tell me, sir, by what right have you forced an entrance into my house?'

'The same by which I should have clung to your boat, if I were drowning. The right of self-preservation.'

'Self-preservation?'

'There's an inch of snow on the ground already,' I replied, briefly; 'and it would be deep enough to cover my body before daybreak.'

He strode to the window, pulled aside a heavy black curtain, and looked out.

'It is true,' he said. 'You can stay, if you choose, till morning. Jacob, serve the supper.'

With this he waved me to a seat, resumed his own, and became at once absorbed in the studies from which I had disturbed him.

I placed my gun in a corner, drew a chair to the hearth, and examined my quarters at leisure. Smaller and less incongruous in its arrangements than the hall, this room contained, nevertheless, much to awaken my curiosity. The floor was carpetless. The white-washed walls were in parts scrawled over with strange diagrams, and elsewhere covered with shelves crowded with instruments, the uses of many of which were unknown to me. On one side of the fireplace stood a bookcase filled with shabby folios; on the other, a small organ, fantastically decorated with painted carvings of mediaeval saints and devils. Through the half-opened door of a cupboard at the further end of the room I saw a long array of geological specimens, surgical preparations, crucibles, retorts, and jars of chemicals; while on the mantelshelf beside me, amid a number of small objects, stood a model of the solar system, a small galvanic battery, and a microscope. Every chair had its burden. Every corner was heaped high with books. The very floor was littered over with maps, casts, papers, tracings, and learned lumber of all conceivable kinds.

I stared about me with an amazement increased by every fresh object upon which my eyes chanced to rest. So strange a room I had never seen before; yet stranger still was its presence in a solitary farmhouse amid these wild and lonely moors! If what I saw aroused a keen curiosity, I was no lest intrigued as to the identity of my host and how he came to be living here. His head was singularly fine; but it was more the head of a poet than of a philosopher. Broad in the temple, prominent over the eyes, and clothed in an unruly shock of perfectly white hair, it had the appeal and much of the ruggedness that characterizes the head of Lüdwig van Beethoven. While I was yet observing him, the door opened, and Jacob brought in the supper. His master then closed his book, rose, and with more courtesy than he had yet shown, invited me to the table.

A dish of ham and eggs, a loaf of brown bread, and a bottle of admirable sherry, were placed before me.

'I have but the homeliest farmhouse fare to offer you, sir,' said my host. 'Your appetite, I trust, will make up for the deficiencies of our larder.'

I had already fallen upon the viands, and now protested, with the enthusiasm of a starving sportsman, that I had never eaten anything so delicious.

He bowed stiffly, and sat down to his own supper, which consisted primitively, of a jug of milk and a basin of porridge. We ate in silence, and when we had done, Jacob removed the tray. I then drew my chair back to the fireside. My host, somewhat to my surprise, did the same, and, turning abruptly towards me, said:

'Sir, I have lived here in strict retirement for three-and-twenty years. During that time I have not seen many unknown faces and I have not read a single newspaper. You are the first stranger who has crossed my threshold for more than four years. Will you favour me with a little information respecting that outer world from which I have parted company so long?'

'Pray interrogate me,' I replied. 'I am willingly at your service.'

He bent his head in acknowledgment; leaned forward, with his elbows resting on his knees and his chin supported in the palms of his hands; stared fixedly into the fire; and proceeded to question me.

His inquiries related chiefly to scientific matters, with the later progress of which, as applied to the practical purposes of life, he was almost wholly unacquainted. No student of science myself, I replied as well as my slight knowledge permitted; but the task was far from easy, and I was much relieved when, passing from interrogation to discussion, he began to formulate his own conclusions upon the facts which I had been attempting to place before him. He talked, and I listened spellbound. Later on I believe he almost forgot my presence, and only thought aloud. I had never heard anything like it then nor since. Familiar with most schools of philosophy, subtle in analysis, bold in generalization, his thoughts were expressed in an uninterrupted stream, and, still leaning forward in the same moody attitude with his eyes fixed upon the fire, wandered from topic to topic, from one speculation to another, like an inspired dreamer. From practical science to mental philosophy; from Watts to Mesmer, from Mesmer to Reichenbach, from Reichenbach to Swedenborg, Spinoza, Condillac, Descartes, Berkeley, Aristotle, Plato, and the Magi and mystics of the East, were transitions which, however bewildering in their variety and scope, seemed easy and harmonious upon his lips as sequences in music. By and by – I forget now by what link of conjecture or illustration – he passed on to that field which lies beyond the boundary of even conjectural philosophy, and reaches no man knows where. He spoke of the soul and its aspirations; of the spirit and its powers; of second sight; of prophecy; of those phenomena which, under the names of ghosts, spectres, and supernatural appearances, have been denied by sceptics and attested by the credulous, of all ages.

'The world,' he said, 'grows hourly more and more sceptical of all that lies beyond its own narrow radius; and our men of science foster the fatal tendency. They condemn as fable all that resists experiment. They reject as false all that cannot be brought to the test of the laboratory or the dissecting-room. Against what superstition have they waged so long and obstinate a war, as against the belief in apparitions? And yet what superstition had maintained its hold upon the minds of men so long and so firmly? Show me any fact in physics, in history, in archaeology, which is supported by testimony so wide and so various. Attested by all races of men, in all ages, and in all climes, by the soberest sages of antiquity, by the rudest savage of today, by the Christian, the Pagan, the Pantheist, the Materialist, this phenomenon is treated as a nursery tale by the philosophers of our century. Circumstantial evidence weighs with them as a feather in the balance. The comparison of cause with effect, however valuable in physical science, is put aside as worthless and unreliable. The evidence of competent witnesses, however conclusive in a court of justice, counts for nothing. He who pauses before he pronounces, is condemned as a trifler. He who believes, is a dreamer or a fool.'

He spoke with bitterness, and, having said thus, relapsed for some minutes into silence. Presently he raised his head from his hands, and added, with an altered voice and manner:

'I, sir, paused, investigated, believed, and was not ashamed to state my convictions to the world. I, too, was branded as a visionary, held up to ridicule by my contemporaries, and excluded from that field of science in which I had laboured with honour during all the best years of my life. These things happened just three-and-twenty years ago. Since then I have lived as you see me living now, and the world has forgotten me, as I have forgotten the world. You now know my history.'

'It is a very sad one,' I murmured, scarcely knowing what to answer.

'It is a very common one,' he replied. 'I have only suffered for the truth, as many a better and wiser man has done before me.'

He rose, as if desirous of ending the conversation, and went over to the window.

'It has ceased snowing,' he observed, as he dropped the curtain and came back to the fireside.

'Ceased!' I exclaimed, starting eagerly to my feet,

'Oh, if it were only possible – but no! It is no use. Even if I could find my way across the moor, I could not walk twenty miles tonight.'

'Walk twenty miles tonight!' repeated my host. 'What are you thinking of?'

'Of my wife,' I replied, impatiently. 'Of my young wife, who does not know that I have lost my way, and who is at this moment, I am sure, in despair over my absence.'

'Where is she?'

'At Dwolding, twenty miles away.'

'At Dwolding,' he echoed, thoughtfully. 'Yes, the distance, it is true, is twenty miles; but – are you that anxious to make the journey before dawn?'

'So very, very anxious, that I would give ten guineas at this moment for a guide and a horse.'

'Your wish can be gratified at less cost,' he said, smiling. 'The night mail from the north, which changes horses at Dwolding, passes within five miles of this spot, and will be due at a certain cross-road in about an hour and a quarter. If Jacob were to go with you across the moor and put you along the old coach-road, you could find your way, I suppose, to where it joins the new one?'

'Easily – gladly.'

He smiled again, rang the bell, gave the old servant his directions, and, taking a bottle of whisky and a wineglass from the cupboard in which he kept his chemicals, said:

'The snow lies deep and it will be difficult walking tonight on the moor. A glass of usquebaugh before you start?'

I would have declined the spirit, but he pressed it on me, and I drank it. It went down my throat like liquid flame and almost took my breath away.

'It is strong,' he said; 'but it will help to keep out the cold. And now you have no time to spare. Good night!'

I thanked him for his hospitality and would have shaken hands with him but that he had turned away before I could make the gesture. In another minute I had traversed the hall, Jacob had locked the outer door behind me, and we were out on the wide white moor.

Although the wind had fallen, it was bitterly cold. Not a star glimmered in the black vault overhead. Not a sound, save the crunch of snow beneath our feet, disturbed the heavy stillness of the night. Jacob, not too well pleased with his mission, ambled along in sullen silence, his lantern in his hand and his shadow at his feet. I followed, with my gun over my shoulder, as little inclined for conversation as himself. My thoughts were full of my late host. His voice still rang in my ears, his eloquence yet held my imagination captive. I remember to this day, with surprise, how my mind, greatly stimulated, retained so much of what he had said, troops of brilliant images, and fragments of splendid reasoning, in the very words he himself had used. Musing thus over what I had heard, and striving to recall a lost link here and there, I strode on at the heels of my guide, absorbed and unobservant. Presently – and it seemed only a few minutes since we had set off – Jacob came to a sudden halt, and said:

'Yon's your road. Keep the stone fence to your right hand and you can't fail to find your way.'

'This, then, is the old coach-road?'

'Ay, 'tis the old coach-road.'

'And how far do I go before I reach the cross-roads?'

'Nigh upon three mile.'

I pulled out my purse, and he became more communicative.

'The road's a fair road enough,' said he, 'for foot passengers; but 'twas over-steep and narrow for the northern traffic. You'll mind where the parapet's broken away, close again' the sign-post. It's never been mended since the accident.'

'What accident?'

'Eh, the night mail pitched right over into the valley

below – a gude fifty feet an' more – just at the worst bit o' road in the whole county.'

'Horrible! Were many lives lost?'

'All. Four were found dead, and t'other two died next morning.'

'How long is it since this happened?'

'Just nine year.'

'Near the sign-post, you say? I will bear it in mind. Good night.'

'Gude night, sir, and thankee.' Jacob pocketed his half-crown, made a faint pretence of touching his hat, and trudged back by the way he had come.

I watched the light of his lantern till it disappeared, and then turned to pursue my way alone. I had not now the slightest cause for concern, for, despite the darkness the line of stone fence showed distinctly enough against the pale gleam of the snow. How silent it seemed now, with only my footsteps to listen to; how solitary! A strange disagreeable sense of loneliness however soon stole over me. I walked faster. I hummed a fragment of a tune. I cast up enormous sums in my head, and accumulated them at compound interest. I did my best, in short, to forget the startling speculations to which I had but just been listening, and, to some extent, I succeeded.

Meanwhile, the night air seemed to become colder and colder, and though I walked fast I found it impossible to keep myself warm. My feet were like ice. I lost sensation in my hands, and grasped my gun mechanically. I even breathed with difficulty, as though, instead of traversing a quiet North-country highway, I were scaling the uppermost heights of some gigantic mountain. This last symptom became presently so distressing that I was forced to stop for a few minutes and lean against the stone fence. As I did so I chanced to look back up the road, and there, to my infinite relief, I saw a distant point of light, like the gleam of an approaching lantern. At first I thought that Jacob had retraced his steps and followed me; but even as the conjecture presented itself, a second light flashed into sight – a light evidently parallel with the first, and approaching at the same rate of motion. It needed no second thought to show me that these must be the carriage-lamps of some private vehicle, though it seemed strange that any such conveyance should take a road no longer used and regarded as dangerous.

There could be no doubt, however, of the fact, for the lamps grew larger and brighter every moment, and I even fancied I could already see the dark outline of the carriage between them. It was coming up very fast, and quite noiselessly, the snow being nearly a foot deep under the wheels.

And now the body of the vehicle became distinctly visible behind the lamps. It looked strangely lofty. A sudden suspicion flashed upon me. Was it possible that I had passed the cross-roads in the dark without observing the sign-post and could this be the very coach which I had come to meet?

No need to ask myself that question a second time, for here it came round the bend of the road, guard and driver, one outside passenger, and four steaming greys, all wrapped in a soft haze of light, through which the lamps blazed out, like a pair of glowing meteors.

I jumped forward, waved my hat, and shouted. The vehicle came down at full speed, and passed me. The coachman pulled up; the guard, muffled to the eyes in capes and comforters, and apparently sound asleep in the rumble, neither answered my hail nor made the slightest effort to dismount; the outside passenger did not even turn his head. I opened the door for myself, and looked in. There were but three travellers inside, so I stepped in, shut the door, slipped into the vacant corner, and congratulated myself on my good fortune.

The atmosphere of the coach seemed, if possible, colder than that of the outer air and was pervaded by a singularly damp and disagreeable smell. I looked round at my fellow-passengers. They were three of them, men, and all silent. They did not seem to be asleep, but each leaned back in his corner of the vehicle, as if absorbed in his own reflections. I attempted to open a conversation.

'How intensely cold it is tonight,' I said, addressing my opposite neighbour.

He lifted his head, looked at me, but made no reply.

'The winter,' I added, 'seems to have begun in earnest.'

Although the corner in which he sat was so dim that I could distinguish none of his features very clearly, I saw that his eyes were still turned full upon me. And yet he spoke no word.

At any other time I should have felt, and perhaps expressed, some annoyance, but at the moment I felt too ill to do either. The icy coldness of the night air had struck a chill to my very marrow, and the strange smell inside the coach was so powerful that it gave me a feeling of intense nausea. I shivered from head to foot, and, turning to my neighbour on the left, I asked if he had any objection to an open window?

He neither spoke nor stirred.

I repeated the question rather more emphatically, but with the same result. Then I lost my patience and let the sash down. As I did so, the leather strap broke in my hand, and I noticed that the glass was covered with a thick coat of mildew, the accumulation, apparently, of years of neglect. My attention being thus drawn to the condition of the coach, I examined it more carefully, and saw by the uncertain light of the outer lamps that it was in the last stage of dilapidation. Every part of it was not only decrepit but in a condition of decay. The sashes splintered at a touch and the leather fittings were encrusted with mould, and literally rotting from the woodwork. The floor was I could see, in a dangerous condition. The vehicle, in fact, was foul with damp, and had evidently been dragged from some outhouse in which it had been mouldering away for years, to do another day or two of duty on the road.

I turned to the third passenger, whom I had not yet addressed, and hazarded one more remark.

'This coach,' I said, 'is in a deplorable condition. The regular mail, I suppose, is under repair?'

He moved his head slowly, and looked me in the face, without speaking a word. I shall never forget that look while I live. I turned cold at heart under it. I tremble even now when I recall it. His eyes glowed with a fiery unnatural lustre and his face was as livid as that of a corpse. His bloodless lips were drawn back as if in the agony of death, and showed the gleaming teeth between.

The words that I was about to utter died upon my lips, and a strange horror – an unspeakable dread – came upon me. My sight had by this time become used to the gloom of the coach, and I could see with tolerable distinctness. I turned to my opposite neighbour. He, too, was looking at me with the same startling pallor in his face and the same awful glitter in his eyes. I passed my hand across my brow. I turned to the passenger on the seat beside my own, and saw – oh, Heaven! how shall I describe what I saw? I saw that he was no living man – that none of them were living men, like myself! A pale phosphorescent light – the light of putrefaction – played upon their awful faces; upon their hair, dank with the dews of the grave; upon their clothes, earth stained and falling to pieces; upon their hands, which were as the hands of corpses long buried. Only their eyes, their terrible eyes, were living; and those eyes were all turned menacingly upon me!

A shriek of terror, a wild, unintelligible cry for help and mercy, burst from my lips as I flung myself against the door and strove in vain to open it.

In that single instant, brief and vivid as a landscape held in the flash of summer lightning, I saw the moon shining down through a rift of stormy cloud – the ghastly sign-post rearing its warning finger by the wayside – the broken parapet – the plunging horses – the black gulf below. The coach reeled like a ship in heavy seas. Then came a mighty crash – a sense of crushing pain – and then darkness.

It seemed as if years had passed when I awoke one morning from a deep sleep and found my wife watching at my bedside. I will not describe the scene that ensued and will tell you, in a few words, the tale she told me with tears of thanksgiving. I had fallen over a precipice, quite close to the junction of the old coach-road and the new, and had only been saved from certain death by lighting upon a deep snowdrift that had accumulated at the foot of the rock beneath. In this snowdrift I was discovered at daybreak by a couple of shepherds, who carried me to the nearest shelter, and brought a surgeon to my aid. He found me in a state of delirium, with a broken arm and a compound fracture of the skull. The letters in my pocket-book showed my name and address; my wife was summoned to nurse me; and, thanks to my youth and robust constitution and to the care I received I survived the dangerous phases of my illness. The place of my fall, I need scarcely say, was precisely that at which a frightful accident had happened to the north mail nine years before.

I never told my wife the fearful events which I have just related to you, but confided in the surgeon who attended me; but he treated the whole adventure as a mere dream born of the fever in my brain. We discussed the affair on several occasions until we found that our differing views provoked too sharp an argument and we never referred to it again. Others may form what conclusions they please – I *know* that twenty years ago I was the fourth passenger inside the Phantom Coach.

Ghosts Come to Hell

Pat Scholer

People who don't believe in ghosts are usually content to say so and pass on to other matters but not dapper, forty-year-old Welsh actor John Heel, now living in Sydney.

Early in his life Heel decided against the existence of ghosts. Since then he has devoted much of his time to proving he took the right line.

During his search for certainty, Heel became a member of England's Ghost Club, an association of people dedicated to coming to grips with Things.

He visited reputedly haunted buildings, confronted invisible barriers, pursued disembodied footsteps, fled from a voice urging him to kill himself, and explored the Great Pyramid of Egypt while leaving his body safe at home in his London flat.

Though these experiences might have shaken another man's disbelief in the supernatural, Heel has stuck to his theory that there's nothing about ghosts that science can't explain, given a little more time.

Ghosts, he insists, are not spirits returned from the

grave, but a type of photograph. Everybody, so he reasons, leaves some impression or image in the atmosphere, and a person under stress leaves a very strong image which someone else may later see and call a ghost.

American scientists, he points out, claim they have developed a time camera, an infra-red device which looks back through time and takes pictures of what it sees. This camera, focused on an empty parade ground, is said to have taken a photograph of soldiers who were there some time previously.

Doesn't this, Heel asks, rather point up his theory that people leave an image in the atmosphere?

Heel would have appreciated having some such device as the time camera along with him on his ghost hunts. It might have come in handy, for instance, in that seventeenth century house in North Wales which was the scene of one of his first encounters with the Unexplained. Heel explored the house with a friend when he was only seventeen.

'The place was in excellent condition, yet it had been vacant for years because it was disturbed,' Heel says in that richly dramatic voice which has interpreted so many roles in the English theatre.

'Ah yes, undoubtedly it was disturbed. Doors opened and shut. Across the staircase there was an invisible barrier so strong that when we tried to break through it we couldn't.'

Would that be the work of a photograph? 'Let's say of – a force,' Heel replies, and his voice drops to a sibilant murmur which is quite unsettling. 'Something had happened in that house. Something – rather horrible, I imagine, had left behind this super-charged atmosphere. Perhaps we disturbed it. Perhaps a sort of electricity caused the doors to open and shut.'

One of Heel's lighter encounters with the supernatural (for lack of a more scientific word) occurred on Snowdon, the highest mountain in Wales.

'This is a story I cannot account for,' Heel admits candidly. 'All I can say is it happened.' And the resonant voice takes up the tale of the Tylwydd Teg.

'The Welsh,' he explains, 'are a romantic and imaginative people. Through the centuries they have cherished the tradition of the Tylwydd Teg – the fairy music of Snowdon. I have heard this music.

'I was staying at the foot of Snowdon. One moonlit night it occurred to me that it was bright enough to climb a little way up the mountain and have a look at the view. I must confess that the thought also came into my mind – "I'll find out about the Tylwydd Teg business".'

By two o'clock in the morning, Heel had climbed some way up Snowdon. He was resting, admiring the moonlit view, when he saw, moving slowly down the mountain, a figure – a misty, wild-looking figure.

It was an old shepherd. 'We greeted each other. And then I said to him, "I've been wondering if there's anything to this Tylwydd Teg business".'

According to Heel, the shepherd told him there certainly was, and if he'd just keep quiet he'd probably hear for himself. 'So we sat whispering for about a quarter of an hour,' Heel relates, 'and then suddenly I heard the music. Clearly, like dozens of tiny, tinkling bells – the fairy music of Snowdon.'

He smiles as if he were still listening to that magical sound. 'Well, after about a quarter of an hour the music died away. I said to the old boy, "I'm privileged, I never thought I'd hear that. Astonishing".'

'The old boy,' however, pointed out that there was little call for astonishment, because after all he had been sitting inside one of the enchanted circles of Snowdon – circles of bracken trodden down by the dancing feet of fairies.

'I looked around,' Heel says, 'and right enough, there was the ring of dead bracken, and I was inside it.' In those circumstances, of course, he declares it was not remarkable that he'd heard the Tylwydd Teg.

Heel was in York, with Emlyn Williams' theatrical company, the next time he tangled with a Something which science has yet to explain. On this occasion the puzzle was set by the shade of a nun, known as the Grey Lady of the Theatre Royal.

According to talk around York, this stage-struck ghost often joined the actors during a performance or stood quietly watching them from the auditorium.

'The walls and foundations of this theatre, which was near York Minster, belonged to an ancient nunnery,' Heel explains. 'Below the stage was the nunnery well, where it was the custom of the artists to throw in a penny and make a wish – I did it myself.

'The stalls bar was one of the most perfect examples in all England of a Norman crypt.

'The backstage entrance was through a long, low, dark, stone tunnel. You felt there was something eerie there. The whole atmosphere was one of foreboding.'

It being wartime when he was in York, Heel was often rostered on fire-watching duty after a show closed. It was on one of these occasions, when he was on duty with a member of the stage crew, that he heard the footsteps of the Grey Lady.

'Everything was quiet. We were having a cup of coffee together,' Heel relates, 'when I heard a sound like the pattering of footsteps in the tunnel. So I said to this chap, "What was that sound?" He said, "Don't worry. Happens all the time. Forget it".'

Heel, as a member of the Ghost Club, was simply not the man to accept advice of that sort. 'The pattering sound crossed the wooden stage. I followed. I couldn't see anybody or anything.

'The footsteps led me up the spiral stairs to the dressing rooms. I knew the doors were locked, yet now they were opening as if at a touch. Lights were going on.

'I followed the steps from one dressing room to another. I followed them down the stairs again, I followed them down the stone passage and right out through the stage door. And there they just faded out on the roadway, in the direction of the Great West Door of York Minster.'

In the following year in another theatre, the Royal in Leicester, he had another supernatural experience.

'The place was about one hundred and twenty-seven years old,' he says. 'I was managing it, as well as acting there. I had so much work to do I often stayed on in the theatre after everyone else had gone.

'I'd never had time to explore the place, so one night after the show finished I thought I'd take a look around. I'd heard there was a lot of furniture stored under the stage and I began with that.

'The furniture turned out to be simply covered with dust. Filthy. I was in evening dress, so I decided to leave it for another time.'

And then, he says, some impulse prompted him to make his way up through the gloom into the network of catwalks and galleries forty feet above the stage.

He explored the fly gallery, from which the scenery was manipulated, and the paint gallery, used by the scenic artists. He was halfway over the catwalk across the proscenium arch when he saw, in the wall next to him, a trapdoor.

He hesitated, then wrenched it open. There, stretching back across the roof of the auditorium, was a huge storeroom strewn with the debris of perhaps a century of super-colossal productions; papier mache columns, urns, tattered costumes, plaster statues mantled in the dust of the years.

Shutting the trapdoor, Heel proceeded along the catwalk, feeling his way through shadow pierced weakly by a small pilot light. 'And now – ' Heel's voice sinks, as he relates the story, 'now came the first and only occasion in all this ghost business that I have been absolutely terrified.

'I began to get a feeling. A very curious feeling. Remember, I was forty feet above the stage. And I heard these words: "Jerry wants you to do it – jump over. Jerry wants you to do it – jump over."'

After a long pause – 'Of course,' Heel says in a normal voice, 'I'm willing to admit I might not really have heard those words, that they might perhaps have existed merely in my subconscious –

'Anyway, I ran. I simply turned and ran. I got out of that theatre as fast as I could.'

Next morning Heel called in the stage manager and the electrician who had worked for years at the Royal and asked them if there were any queer stories about the theatre.

Well, they said, there was a stagehand who went berserk. He'd rushed into the fly gallery, put a rope around his neck and thrown himself over. Now, what was his name again? Of course – Jerry.

They mentioned that there was the black shadow which sometimes appeared when they were working late. It had a habit of moving across the spotlight, blotting it out, they said. The shadow carried with it a clammy, chill feeling and a nasty smell.

'But although I stayed back with those men several times, hoping to see the shadow,' Heel says, 'I admit it never appeared when I was there. From which you might gather that I'm not the type to claim to see things when I don't.'

Another case about which Heel gives a fairly detached report was that of St Margaret's vicarage, Leicester. He remembers discussing this case with the Bishop of Leicester as they waited for their respective trains.

'When I first caught sight of the Bishop,' Heel tells, 'I noticed there was something odd about him. Then I realized what it was. He was not wearing his gaiters.

'Well, I greeted him in the usual way – "How d'you do, my lord, long time no see", and so on – and then I got around to the subject of St Margaret's vicarage. I knew he'd arranged to visit the place and I asked him how he'd got on.

'Well, he was a broad-minded man, charming – so many bishops aren't, but he was. He said to me, "Johnny, you'll have noticed I'm not wearing my gaiters". So I said, "Why yes, my lord".

'He said, "Johnny, between you and me, at that vicarage I was scared right out of them".'

One of the disturbing phenomena of St Margaret's was a phosphorescent green light which would fill a closed room. Once the door was opened the light would fade, after which the air would be rent by a sound which might be described as a screaming laugh – or, perhaps, as a laughing scream.

Then of course there was the black-robed figure which walked up and down a flagged stone passageway – doing little harm, actually, by comparison with another figure in white which kept turning up in the staff quarters and frightening away the servants.

The vicar's harassed wife had to manage a household where cloths were pulled off tables by invisible hands (or something), sheets and blankets were whisked off beds and made to disappear in front of her, and cups and saucers took off from their shelves and sailed away into nothingness.

'Finally she'd lose her temper,' Heel recalls, 'and shout out, "Oh, for heaven's sake give me back my things." Then back they'd come, you know. Mysteriously, they'd all be returned to her, and the house would be quiet for a while.'

Heel is certain that most of the phenomena at St Margaret's were due to a poltergeist – defined in the dictionary as 'a noisy ghost, a spirit assumed as the explanation of rappings and other unexplained noises.'

'Poltergeists,' Heel says, 'are two a penny.'

In his opinion, though, they are not spirits, but

manifestations of something in the mind of an adolescent, usually a girl. The adolescent is seldom aware of the poltergeist's behaviour, which often suggests that of a disembodied bogie.

'Poltergeists can be horrible, evil,' Heel insists. 'But also they're silly. I mean, where's the point in picking up a chair, whirling it around and throwing it down again? Ridiculous.

'There was the case of the Battersea poltergeist. I saw the girl myself, just sitting there quietly watching television, unaware of this poltergeist thing operating all around her – hats flying, tapping on walls, a piece of chalk drawing a face on a blind.

'Oh yes. I watched that piece of chalk myself. Moving through the air, drawing, and nothing holding it.'

Heel did not return to the vicarage to investigate the poltergeist of St Margaret's. The Bishop asked him not to because he disliked the publicity which often attended an investigation by Ghost Club members.

Heel's relations with other churchmen in Leicester were not always so happy, especially after he produced James Bridie's 'Mr Bolfry,' a play which brings the devil on to the stage to claim the soul of a parson.

Cast as the parson, Heel evolved what he feels was one of his most spectacular make-ups to turn himself into the crabbed old churchman. 'I had to take the play off after three nights,' Heel told us. 'The church people said it was sacrilegious.'

In 1951 Heel moved to London and because of an acute accommodation shortage, he and his wife and mother had to settle into shabby lodgings. It was then Heel read that the Dover Museum wished to sell an Egyptian mummy which had been in a room damaged in an air raid.

'I wrote,' Heel recalls. 'Purely for a joke, of course. I was invited down to Dover, however, and found that the mummy had lost some of its bandages – it seemed that workmen had searched it for ornaments – but I was impressed by the fine preservation of the body.

'I made an offer for it. An absurd offer, really – £3. And the museum jumped at it.

'When I recovered from the shock it seemed to me extremely peculiar that the museum should be glad to dispose of the mummy for such a small sum. However, I arranged with a road cartage firm to pick up the mummy and deliver it to my digs. Their charge was 25s.

'That made £4 5s. altogether for a mummy – a twenty-one-year-old boy, according to the museum, a priest of Isis of 2,500 years ago.

'Later I received a letter from the museum saying that a chap living in south London had been interested in the mummy, and would like to meet its new owner. So I wrote to this man – Stanley Forsythe – and he invited me to go to see him.'

Forsythe explained to Heel that, as a child, he'd spent many happy hours in the Dover Museum looking at the mummies and so he had a particular interest in the specimen Heel had acquired.

'I'm going to make you an offer,' Forsythe told Heel. 'At the top of this house there's a furnished flat, five rooms, self-contained. I'll let you have it for 35s. a week if you will bring your mummy with you, store it in the basement, and allow me to help with the restoration.'

That was the way Heel acquired a comfortable flat and a famous address – 34 Lancaster Road, South Norwood. It was at No. 34 that such celebrities as Sir Oliver Lodge and Sir Arthur Conan Doyle had attended seances. 'That house,' Heel says, 'was literally saturated with psychic emanations.'

Forsythe, the landlord, turned out to be a writer with a side interest in Egyptology and anatomy. After sessions in the basement cleaning up the coffin and re-winding the outer bandages of the mummy, Forsythe became convinced that the body was not that of a twenty-one-year-old boy but of a girl of about sixteen. In the hope that spirits would confirm his theory, he arranged a seance.

For the occasion, the mummy was carried upstairs to the dining-room. There, under the bright light of an electric chandelier, the seance proceeded in the presence of reporters from the London papers, three spiritualists, Forsythe and Heel, and two friends.

The medium who conducted the seance over the Egyptian mummy was, in Heel's words, 'a young woman who kept a confectionery shop and couldn't even tell you who Tutankhamen was.

'Yet after she'd gone into a trance,' Heel relates, 'she came straight over to me and in a strange voice, the voice of an old, old man, described a temple. It seemed to be a cross between a Greek and Roman building, and I couldn't make much sense out of it.

'The voice said a girl had died and had paid a terrible price for a crime committed. Then the voice changed into that of a young girl. And this is the message I received (I make no comment on it):

'"My name is Katrina. I was accounted fair in the eyes of the Pharaoh and all the land of Egypt. I died and was buried. I sinned against my Pharaoh and I paid the price.

'"I was a priestess in the temple of Orkon. You have saved my body from destruction and so long as you shall keep me safe within these walls I will do harm to all those who would hurt the dwellers within these walls. Protect me, preserve me. In life I suffered acutely from a painful disease."

'A few weeks later a young doctor said he'd like to examine the mummy and I gave him permission.

'Somehow the newspapers got hold of the story. My word, you know, it's a good job I've got a sense of humour, otherwise I might easily have lost my temper. The heading the *Sunday Dispatch* gave the story was, "He is sending his mummy to see a doctor."

‘Ah well. Three days later I received the doctor’s report. It said that the mummy was the remains of a girl of sixteen, that there were not sufficient internal organs to give a definite cause of death, and that she had suffered from spondylitis.

‘In other words, the medium’s Katrina voice had been right in claiming the body as a girl’s, and right about her suffering from a painful disease.’

Confirmation of statements made in the medium’s old-man voice came, Heel adds, from Egyptologist Sir Alan Gardiner. He wrote that the mummy dated from the Graeco-Roman period of Egyptian history and probably from the reign of Osorkon II or III.

Later, despite her promises to be nice to her hosts, Katrina began to misbehave. Heel’s mother insisted she had seen queer shadows moving about in the basement.

‘I suspected something was disturbing the dust so as a test I spread powdered cement over the floor. I locked the door so that nobody could go in. Later, I inspected the place. The dust had been disturbed. Then, lights began to go on and off in our flat. We began to hear footsteps. One afternoon they crossed the room behind the settee where my wife and I were sitting.’

All this indicated to Heel that Katrina must be dissatisfied with life in a basement, so he brought her upstairs and gave her a room of her own in his flat. Sure enough, the disturbances ceased.

‘But then a very curious thing happened,’ he says. ‘I spent all one night wandering, so it seemed, inside the Great Pyramid of Egypt.

‘Everything was clear, as real as anything I’m looking at now. I seemed to be searching for somebody. I felt I wanted to tell them something.

‘I said to my wife in the morning, “I’ve had a wonderful time – I’ve spent the entire night in the Great Pyramid. I seemed to be looking for somebody.” Of course she laughed – “Looking for your mummy, were you?”

'Now, nobody else heard what I said. Yet when I came home that evening I received a note left by my landlord's wife.

'She had written, "I have a strange story to tell you. Last night I dreamed I was in the Great Pyramid of Egypt. I was looking for you and couldn't find you. It seemed I had something to tell you about your mummy."

'Well, that shocked my wife pretty badly.'

It was rather a relief to Mrs Heel to leave the mummy behind when, in February, 1958, she and her husband emigrated to Australia.

In his new country, Heel has maintained his interest in the disturbed images usually referred to as ghosts. His investigations have led him to a suspected poltergeist or two, but there's really been nothing to come up to his experiences in Britain.

'There are simply no very ancient buildings here,' he points out. 'No crumbling arches. None of those marvellous ruins.

'Though, of course,' he adds thoughtfully, 'It isn't strictly necessary for a house to be old to be haunted.

'Why, in Croydon, England, it happened in a new pair of semi-detached red brick council houses. The tenants had been in them only a few weeks when the trouble started. They were haunted by a crying baby.

'This baby just cried and cried. You could hear it from the roadway. You could even pinpoint the spot in the room where the noise came from. But you just couldn't see any baby.

'In the end, the tenants of both the houses moved out.

'Mind you,' Heel adds, 'that's not to say there was a ghost. No doubt there is some perfectly rational explanation. I'm sure there is. And one of these days, science will find it.'

Wages of Envy

Mark Bartholomeusz

Juse Appuhamy, Sinhalese, never liked those who talked too much. Unnecessary speech, he felt, was a sign that the speaker was a man of words, rather than deeds. So as a golden rule, more or less, he minded his own business, kept himself to himself, worked like a galley slave at his job of selling vegetables at the neighbouring fairs, and looked after his family with commendable zeal.

As a result of his labours over the years, he slowly but surely began to thrive. One day he found that he was able to afford the money to buy a new cart and even more important, a fine, sturdy bull, to take his produce to market.

Most of Juse Appuhamy's neighbours in the Ceylon village, where he lived, hated to see him perched on top of his fully laden new cart, driving his bull to market with the arrogance of a king. It irked them to think that Juse Appuhamy who had started life as a labourer, like many of them, working in the rice fields for others, had over the years become successful. There was a time, they recalled, when he could hardly afford a rag to his back.

But now he always wore a well laundered shirt and a new sarong.

They regarded with envy his neat little tiled cottage with its even neater compound, swept regularly every day by Ran Menika, Juse's wife. Every bit as industrious as her husband, she, too, was careful of her appearance even when she was busy in the kitchen. The couple's detractors preferred to ignore the fact that it was their own indolence that had kept them poor. Neither would they admit that Juse Appuhamy and his wife had thrived because of their own efforts. Rarely did their day begin later than cocks-crow and the couple's three healthy children were a credit to their parents.

While the rest of the village slept, Juse would be feeding his bull and preparing for his daily round to the outlying districts.

Meanwhile Ran Menika – so named because of her ran or golden complexion – would start baking the hoppers which Juse relished as though they were the rarest delicacies. She always felt that her toil was well worthwhile, when she saw with what relish her husband ate the meal she had prepared for him. On rare occasions he would even tell her, quietly but with a tenderness she was quick to recognize:

'There is not a woman in this village, Menika, who can bake a better hopper or make a finer coconut sambol.'

Ran Menika would pause in her work for a moment, glance at her husband, as if to remind herself of how handsome he was, and say:

'It's your belly talking again.'

Juse would answer with a smile, 'No, that's not quite true. I am sure you know it isn't.'

So while Juse Appuhamy and his wife prospered, there grew between them and the villagers a veritable wall of resentment. Among the most hostile was Juse's immediate neighbour, Marthelis, a thin, characterless man who lived with his wife and family on three acres of land which had been given to him many years ago by the government. Now, Marthelis had allowed more than half of his acreage to be reclaimed by the jungle and his attempts to grow coconuts and vegetables on the remainder were only half-hearted. He preferred to spend too much of this time earning easy money by selling an illicit brew to the villagers and using most of this income to challenge all-comers to a game of cards called 'Buruwa'.

He was not a very good card player though, and lost more often than he won. His wife, Prema, an unkempt creature with hard eyes and sunken cheeks, had truly little to be happy about. She shared with her husband and children a broken-down hut the roof of which leaked badly whenever it rained.

Every time Marthelis or his wife looked towards the opposite compound and saw the neat reliable red tiles on their neighbours' roof, their envy increased.

Prema especially, by that queer logic peculiar to villagers, began to feel that their poverty was due, in some inexplicable way to their neighbours. Never for a moment did she ascribe it to her husband's feckless ways; for strangely enough, she cared for him despite the scant attention he gave her or the children. One night it rained so heavily that in no time at all the hut was full of little pools of water. Prema's two small daughters had hardly a place that was dry to sleep in and began to cry and whimper. In desperation Prema drugged them to sleep with a herbal concoction well known to the villagers and placed them on a mat in the one dry place in the room. When they finally dozed off to sleep she joined her husband, who sat quietly smoking a beedi (a rolled leaf like tobacco).

For a long time neither spoke. They were both deep in their own thoughts. The rain continued its steady murmur for a while and then slowly dwindled to a drizzle. Prema at length unburdened herself of her thoughts.

'I know who has brought us all this bad luck over the years,' she said dolefully.

'Who?' asked Marthelis innocently, though half suspecting the answer.

'Who else but that filthy woman in the next plot,' said Prema viciously. 'It isn't natural for our family to go on having this bad luck for so long. Yes, for fifteen years I have been your wife and I haven't even a tiled roof to show for it. I live in the same mud hut as you brought me to when I first got married. Only now it leaks a lot more.'

'So how could that woman cause our ill-luck?' asked Marthelis.

'Aiyo,' said Prema. 'As though you don't know.'

'Do you think they have done something?'

'I don't think they have done something. I know it.'

Marthelis' latent hatred towards his neighbours allured his interest in what his wife was saying.

'How do you know for certain?' he asked quietly.

'I went to the Pusari (priest) this morning at the shrine in the forest.'

'You went to see the Pusari?'

'Yes.'

'Alone?'

'Yes.'

'You shouldn't have done it,' said Marthelis. 'Not when you have a husband to go with you.'

'When a woman has a husband who plays cards for most of the day,' said Prema, with a trace of annoyance, 'she must learn to do things for herself.'

Marthelis merely took a long pull at his beedi. For a few moments there was silence. But his curiosity got the better of him.

'What did the Pusari say?' he asked nonchalantly.

'He went into a trance first before the shrine to his God and then the God spoke through him.'

'I know. I know all that,' said Marthelis impatiently, wondering why his wife had to waste his time with all these very familiar details. 'What I want to know is what did the God say?'

Prema came to the point at last.

'In a deep voice which seemed to come from his belly, he said that a tall, fair, well dressed woman with a mole on her right cheek, living almost next to our property, had buried a charm in our garden.'

'Charm!' Marthelis could not conceal the fear he felt when he heard the dreaded word.

'Yes,' said Prema. 'And who else but Ran Menika? Is she not as the God described her, even to the mole on her right cheek?'

Marthelis paused for a moment deep in thought. 'The God cannot be wrong,' he said at length, 'if he described our neighbour so exactly. Where did he say the charm was buried?'

'It is the kind of charm which no one can ever find and was buried many years ago.'

'No one can ever find?' Marthelis really was alarmed.

'Yes. But don't be frightened. The Pusari also said that the power of this charm could be cut.'

'By whom?'

'By him, of course.'

Marthelis sighed with relief. He felt as though a great load had been lifted from his chest. 'I suppose,' he said, finally, 'we will have to take him an offering of some kind when next we go to see him.'

'Yes,' said Prema. 'When I went for water this morning at the wewa (lake) I asked Aunt Marthina what I would have to take, apart from the nine limes and the husked coconut that the Pusari asked me to bring for the cutting ceremony and she said that all we needed was a two rupee note.'

About a week after this conversation Marthelis and Prema both found that they were constantly thinking of what had been done to them by their neighbours, to bring them under the spell of an evil demon, and their consequent misfortunes and poverty. It rankled so much within them that they could not help but speak about it to others in the village. Very soon, the revelation of the Pusari concerning Juse and his wife became known to everybody.

Villagers nodded their heads wisely and said, 'We always knew that those two were not people to be trusted. The Forest God is never wrong. This explains why they have far more money than the rest of us. They are people who dabble in charms and are able to secure the aid of the demons to help them prosper.' Prema and her husband agreed whole-heartedly. Even the handful of acquaintances, who had no grudge against Juse and his wife, began to regard them as something of a threat. They didn't want too many dabblers in black magic in their midst.

The couple had no inkling of the evil rumours that daily were whispered behind their backs. Juse, of course, was aware of the part played by gossip in village life, but he would hardly have believed it even if he had been warned of the dangerous situation that was developing.

Perhaps the last straw was when Juse acquired a handsome transistor set and Prema and her husband heard the sound of music from their neighbour's compound. They were furious as they huddled together in their miserable hovel and, there and then, decided they would no longer delay their visit to the Pusari so that the evil spell which had bound them to poverty for so long should be destroyed for ever.

A visit to the Pusari was not an easy undertaking but Prema and Marthelis were determined to bring about a change in their fortunes or ensure, at least, the ruin of Juse Appuhamy and his wife. So, one morning, they packed a loaf of bread and some bananas into a cloth bag and also took with them a husked coconut, nine limes and a note worth two rupees as offerings.

Shortly after starting their journey they left the road that led out of the village and took to a path through the thick forest. They had five miles to trudge before they came to the shrine. Marthelis thought the journey would never end. He was afraid of the great forest and the silence and gloom. The sun overhead could not penetrate the barrier created by the height of the enormous trees and every shadow filled Marthelis with foreboding. He wondered what he would do if a leopard crossed their path and could hardly repress a shudder on remembering that his wife not long ago had come here alone. The only sign of wild life was that of an occasional jungle fowl which darted into the undergrowth as they approached.

After about two hours they finally came to a clearing at the end of which stood a great tree under which was a crude little structure built of stone and cement and consisting of two rooms. In one of them the Pusari slept, ate and lived, in the other he communicated his revelations from the deity.

As Marthelis and Prema approached the Pusari was intoning a litany before the God he worshipped, symbolized by a massive black image only vaguely suggesting a human outline. On each side of the idol, which stood upon an altar or stone shelf, stood jars containing smouldering joss sticks. Streamers of smoke coiled and uncoiled as they burned, radiating a sickly sweet perfume. At the foot of the image a large flame burned steadily in the clay receptacle filled with oil. Behind the flame was a mirror which appeared to glow eerily as it reflected the rays from the flame.

The Pusari appeared to sense that Prema and Marthelis were watching him from the entrance. Unhurriedly he concluded his devotions and came out to meet his visitors.

'So you've come,' he said quietly addressing Prema rather than her husband.

'Yes,' said Prema, shifting uneasily.

'I'm glad you have brought your husband with you. It will be easier for me to cut the power of the charm.'

Marthelis glanced at the Pusari but was too awed to speak to a man said to have power over spirits and demons. The priest had a strong, bony face and a commanding presence.

'Have you brought the limes?' he asked.

'Yes,' said Prema.

'Give them to me,' he said.

Prema rummaged within the cloth bag which still hung from her husband's neck, brought out the limes and gave them to him.

'Have you brought the husked coconut?' asked the Pusari again.

This time it was Marthelis who answered. 'Yes,' he said, and extracted the coconut from his bag. The Pusari took the coconut without a word and re-entered the shrine room.

Prema and Marthelis followed quietly behind him. The Pusari placed the limes and the coconut on a side of the altar and then he took a red sash which lay there and tied it round his waist. All he wore below the sash was a white cloth which extended up to his knees. His hairy chest was bare of clothing and was streaked horizontally with markings of ash.

'I shall start praying to the God,' he said quietly.

Prema thought the whiteness of his eyes was startling and so was the blackness of his face, which was also streaked with ash. His reddish brown beard like the hair on his head was matted. For a moment she felt frightened in his presence.

The ascetic seemed to sense her fear. 'Now,' he said, 'I want you to calm yourself and to be silent. Your husband too. The great god of the forest will come only if you deserve his aid.' With these words he clasped his palms together, bowed his head and began to mumble something in a slow monotone.

Neither Prema nor Marthelis could understand what he said. Gradually the priest's voice rose from a whisper to a full-throated call while, at the same time, the upper part of his body began to sway from side to side.

Marthelis and Prema watched intently the weird movement of the Pusari's body. Quite suddenly he became convulsed and his body began vibrating at tremendous speed. His words became a meaningless babel and with each vibration there was a report like a pistol shot; so that ultimately Prema and Marthelis both felt as though the room was filled with the staccato rattle of some curious machine. The noise ceased as suddenly as it had begun and with it all movement by the Pusari himself. A deathly silence filled the room. The ascetic turned slowly away from the image to face Prema and Marthelis.

Prema couldn't repress a shudder when she saw the ascetic's eyes. They were gazing at her and yet through her. Then he slowly raised his hand and placed it on her forehead. He spoke now in a deep voice, so deep thought Prema, that it couldn't possibly belong to a human being.

'You and your husband have suffered greatly,' he said in clear intelligible Sinhalese. 'But the God of the Forest will bring your sufferings to an end.'

Prema felt as though a strange force was radiating from his fingers and coursing through her whole body. She was quite convinced that the God himself was talking. The ascetic touched Marthelis' forehead too in a similar manner. He turned slowly towards the altar and took one of the limes and then a knife. Resting the lime on Prema's head he cut it gently. For a moment he gazed at the two halves of the lime and then threw them on the floor.

Once again Prema and Marthelis heard the priest speak strangely as if the words of another were being transmitted through him.

'Not till a seed within the lime is cut exactly in half is the spell that binds you to poverty destroyed,' it said.

With this pronouncement the ascetic took another lime

from his altar and this time cut it over the head of Marthelis. Once again the seeds were whole and intact. He continued the ceremony using the remaining limes over the heads of Prema and her husband in turn. But every time the seeds remained intact. Prema and Marthelis had almost given up hope when he came to the eighth lime. This time he severed the lime in two over Marthelis' head.

'Ah,' intoned the ascetic. 'The seed has been cut exactly in half. The God of the Forest has destroyed the spell. Go back to your hut. You will no more be under its evil influence.'

Both Prema and Marthelis felt at that moment as though a tremendous burden had been lifted from their spirits. They were overjoyed at their reprieve but there was hatred in their hearts for the people who had kept them poor.

The ascetic turned again towards the image and with head bowed low started to pray. Once more his body began to vibrate violently, but this time there were no staccato sounds. Gradually the rapid movement of the body ceased and he seemed to become his usual self again.

His chest was bathed with sweat as he came up to Prema and Marthelis and spoke to them in his normal voice. They could hardly believe that this was the same Pusari who had spoken to them earlier.

'You have a long way to go now, haven't you?' he asked casually.

'Not too far,' said Prema making light of the situation.

'Do not worry about the future,' he said.

But Prema had made up her mind that she would do something much more positive than await the arrival of better times. She would take her revenge for all that had been done to them. Yes, she was going to visit Malhamy the famous sorcerer who lived in the village next to their own. She would seek his aid to bring misfortune upon Ran Menika and her husband. When she whispered her thoughts to her husband he fully agreed. So with a final nod to the ascetic they left the shrine in the forest. But before they did so they dropped a two rupee note into the bowl kept at the entrance for the offerings of those who came for assistance.

For a few days after the visit to the forest shrine, Prema was aware of a great sense of relief; that oppressive burden of continued poverty which weighed down the spirits of both her and her husband seemed to become lighter. Even Marthelis no longer felt as despondent as he once did about his domestic affairs. Both he and Prema decided that it was the power of the Forest God, wielded through the agency of the Pusari, that had brought them this change in spirit; this feeling that all would be well in the future.

But after about a week, doubts began to nag them. As long as Ran Menika was alive and capable of doing something to them again she was a threat to their security. It was not that they doubted the Pusari's assurances but it seemed like folly not to see Malhamy the Kattadiya (sorcerer) at once. They could tell him what the God had revealed to them through the ascetic and ask for a charm with which to take their revenge.

No sooner they had decided on this trip than they made the journey to the village in which Malhamy lived. It wasn't more than ten miles away and it cost very little by bus from their own home.

Malhamy, contrary to what Prema expected of him, was not the thin, diabolic sorcerer with deep set penetrating eyes that she had imagined. He was a fat, hairy chested man with a great round belly and a face as full as a ripe melon. His eyes twinkled good-naturedly as he stood barefoot on the veranda of his home, clad only in a sarong.

What was even more surprising was that his home was quite different from the majority of mud huts in their village. It was built of brick, neatly white-washed, and had a roof of red tiles. A radio set stood ornamentally in the principal room and there was even a carpet on the veranda floor. A large Ford Prefect stood outside the porch and Malhamy had obviously climbed from humble origins to become one of the more prosperous people in the village.

At first, despite the twinkle in his eye, Prema and Marthelis were awed by the signs of opulence they saw. But Malhamy soon put them at their ease.

'Sit down,' he said in hearty manner, rubbing his naked paunch with two fat palms.

The feeling of awe soon thawed and Marthelis even succeeded in smiling as he took a seat on one of the upright chairs placed along the veranda. Prema followed suit.

Malhamy sat down on another easy chair opposite his clients and began to talk.

'Now,' he said, smiling broadly, 'what is your trouble?'

As usual Prema did most of the talking. 'Our neighbours buried a kodivinia (charm) in our garden many years ago,' she said.

'Kodivinia!' Malhamy had ceased to smile.

'Yes,' said Prema.

'How do you know they did this?'

'The God of the Forest told us. We've had bad luck for fifteen years.'

Malhamy nodded his head as she spoke. These were not the first clients to come to him with revelations from the famous Pusari.

'The God of the Forest is rarely wrong,' he said. 'Well, what do you want me to do?'

'We want you to help us to take our revenge,' said Prema.

'Do you want your neighbours to die?'

'No,' said Marthelis promptly. 'We do not desire their death.'

'Do you want them to be harassed by spirits or demons so that they can never prosper again?'

'Yes,' said Prema. 'If you can do that, specially to Ran Menika the woman mainly responsible for our misery, we will be amply revenged. It is time her pride was humbled.'

'It is not a difficult matter,' said Malhamy. 'But you will have to assist me.'

'We will do anything you ask,' said Prema.

'Very well,' said Malhamy. 'Bring me a three by four inch sheet of copper leaf tomorrow and leave it with me. I shall require also the names of your neighbours, both wife and husband, and their birth dates if you happen to know them. If you don't it won't matter. A charm is generally more effective however, when used on significant occasions such as birthdays. I will charm the copper leaf and then return it so that all you've got to do is bury it somewhere near your neighbours' dwelling. If Ran Menika walks over the buried charm at any time it will take effect.

'Within two weeks she will be so completely in the grip of the power invoked by the charm that she will become the victim of terrifying nightmares. Illness will overcome her and, for as long as the demon continues to haunt their home, your neighbours will experience nothing but despair and misfortune.'

Malhamy ceased talking and looked intently at his clients, trying to fathom the impact of his words. Marthelis was plainly a little scared, now that he began to see the implications of his mission. But Prema smiled as she asked, 'Are you sure all this will come to pass?'

Malhamy laughed. 'I haven't been known as the most powerful Kattadiya in these parts for nothing,' he said. 'People come all the way from the big city of Colombo to this remote village to see me.'

Prema remained thoughtful. Malhamy, she reflected, lived in great comfort and he could hardly have succeeded in doing so all these years on a false reputation.

'I will bring you the copper leaf tomorrow,' she said, 'and also the information you require. But how much will we have to pay you?'

'I will accept payment only if my charm is successful,' said Malhamy, smiling broadly again. 'Of course rich people from the big towns sometimes pay me as much as five hundred rupees for a successful kodivinia.'

Prema started. Five hundred rupees was a fortune. But the sorcerer soon allayed her fears.

'Don't be dismayed,' he said, benignly. 'From people who are villagers like myself I very rarely accept more than fifty rupees.'

Marthelis shifted uneasily in his seat while Prema was silent. Even fifty rupees was a large sum to people as poor as themselves.

Malhamy seemed to read their thoughts. 'I can see that even fifty rupees would be too much for you,' he said. 'Very well, I shall do this for you as a special favour for thirty rupees. Only I don't want you to mention this to anyone in your village.'

'Hondhemai,' (we agree) said Prema and Marthelis, together. 'For that price we are willing to bind ourselves to pay you.'

Malhamy's face creased into a happy smile. 'Now you must remember,' he said, 'that this is a special favour. For those who really cannot afford I don't believe in charging sinful prices.'

Prema and Marthelis returned to their village after their audience with the sorcerer. It wasn't easy for them to secure the necessary information about the exact date of birth of their neighbour Menika. But after some delicate enquiries, made so skilfully that nobody suspected her motives, Prema finally managed to learn the details. The next day, armed with this information she bought the necessary copper leaf from the village goldsmith and took the bus to Malhamy's place, accompanied by her husband.

A week later Malhamy returned the copper leaf to his clients. The plain surface of the leaf was now etched on either side with two charts consisting of squares. Within each square were strange symbols, like birds or reptiles' numbers and occasional letters from the Sinhala alphabet. What these meant neither Prema nor Marthelis could fathom.

Prema took the copper leaf from the sorcerer and handled it gently as though it was some precious metal.

'We are very grateful to you,' she said.

'We will let you know if it is successful,' said Marthelis.

'It should succeed,' said Malhamy, in a sinister tone. 'It is now invested with the power of the Yaksa Lokey.'

Prema almost dropped the charm when she heard the words which meant 'Demon World'.

'Don't worry,' said Malhamy reassuringly. 'You can safely hold it in your palm. It only works against those whom it is intended to harm.'

There was nothing more for Prema and Marthelis to do but return to their hut and wait for nightfall. They were both determined to put their plan into action at the earliest moment. Fortunately it was a moonless night and after one o'clock, while the whole village slept, they could bury the charm unobserved.

Marthelis was the first to suggest a suitable place. 'Let's bury it at the entrance to their veranda,' he said, as he and Prema stood in their own doorway, about to set out on their mission.

'No,' said Prema, after a little thought. 'It's too close to their rooms. Somebody might hear us digging. I think it would be better if we buried it right opposite their main gate. Ran Menika goes to market daily and she is bound to walk over the charm.'

Marthelis thought there was sense in what she suggested. So taking a little torch, a garden fork, and of course, the charm, he and his wife walked quietly through their own front garden till they came to the main road. A few yards walk down this road brought them to the gateway of their neighbours' home.

Marthelis soon got down to digging a hole. It wasn't a difficult task as the soil was soft and sandy. When he reached a depth of a foot or so he buried the charm and then filling up the hole with earth, he covered the traces of his deed with the fine grained sand that formed the outer surface of the soil.

'Nobody will suspect that a charm has been buried here,' said Prema, approvingly, as she flashed the torchlight and examined the surface of the earth. Marthelis rose with a grunt. He too, was well pleased. It was time to return to their own hut and await developments.

They were about to do so when they heard a sudden, furtive rustle. It came from the bushes which stood on either side of the main gate. Prema and Marthelis were both startled. Had they been observed? For a few seconds they stood quite still but nothing happened. Prema switched on the torch and played the light around and then sighed with relief. All they saw was the rear of a rabbit darting away into the darkness.

Juse Appuhamy and his wife meanwhile remained entirely unaware of the sinister scheme of their neighbours. Juse drove his vegetable cart to the market, as was his custom, while his wife, Ran Menika, fulfilled her daily chores with her usual thoroughness.

In the evenings at about five o'clock, when she'd finished washing the two younger of her children at the well, she would take her shopping bag and go to the village store to buy her provisions for the next day. Her eldest daughter, now close upon thirteen years in age, looked after the two younger children, until she returned.

Now this was a routine that Prema was well aware of

and, ever since the night the charm was buried, she began to keep watch at her window waiting for something dramatic to happen.

But for about two weeks nothing unusual took place. Prema, whose desire to harm her neighbours had long become a mania with her, felt her hatred of Ran Menika more unbearable than ever with every day that passed without event.

'May lightning strike the bitch,' she'd swear, to herself, as she saw Ran Menika return daily from shopping, her bag laden with provisions and none the worse for the charm. She seemed to walk proudly, like a queen, through the gateway, as if to announce to the whole village that nothing in the world would ever break her spirit or that lovely slender body of hers so neatly encased in its close fitting jacket. When Prema compared her own shabby and dirty dress with that of Ran Menika the contrast was so great that she spat through the window in spite.

One night Ran Menika went to bed as usual after tucking her three children to sleep. As she sank on to her comfortable mattress she snuggled up to her husband, Juse, who was already snoring and let her thoughts drift. It was good to be sleeping on a mattress, she thought. How many villagers could boast of a nice solid bed and a mattress? She remembered the first years of her marriage when she had nothing more than a mat to sleep on. Ah, it was good to have a husband like Juse, a hard-working honest man who had provided her and the children with all their needs. It was worth loving and being loved by him. She didn't regret the many sacrifices she had made in the way of clothes and even food just to see him happy, with more money to improve his business and now they were about the most flourishing couple in the village.

The flame from the kerosene lamp on the table by their bed cast its ray over Juse's face. His hair was beginning to turn grey she noticed. Poor man; he worked very hard and now time was beginning to show its marks. But his body was still bronzed and sinewy and tough. His face, though ever so slightly wrinkled beneath the eyes, exuded confidence. Yes. He was still handsome. He was her man.

As these thoughts passed through her mind, Ran Menika felt a strange sense of warmth, security and above all tenderness. Slowly she sank into sleep.

After about an hour of dreamless sleep she began to enter a strange world. She was in a dark and dismal forest with long overhanging creepers and she was walking alone through an animal track which seemed to stretch endlessly into the distance. She passed a shrine under a huge tree and she espied an aged ascetic mumbling before a little effigy. She kept on walking. Elephants and leopards began to pad behind her, following, following all the time. She tried to run but couldn't. The track ahead of her became gloomier and gloomier. She was filled with panic as the animals kept up their pursuit and she made a final despairing effort to run, when she saw a little hut standing isolated on a side of the track. With a tremendous effort she got to the door of the hut and pulled at its handle with every ounce of strength in her body. The door burst open and she saw . . . the dead, staring eyes of her husband, whose body was sprawled on the floor, with a serpent sliding over him. She screamed as she reached despairingly for the body of her husband . . .

Juse Appuhamy woke up with a start when he heard his wife's cries and he found her writhing on the bed clutching desperately at him. He caught her firmly by the arm and jolted her into awareness. Her body was trembling and hot with perspiration. She took one look at her husband's face. heaved a huge sigh of relief and rested her head upon his chest.

'What was it, Sudha?' (darling) he asked, tenderly as he took her in his arms.

'I had an awful dream that you were dead,' she whispered, as a fresh tremor passed through her whole body. 'It was terrible.'

The next day Ran Menika was much too busy to worry about her dream of the previous night. There were so many things to be done in the house for her husband and children that she hardly noticed the passing of time as one chore followed another.

When the evening was far gone she went to the store once again for provisions. About half an hour later dusk began to settle over the village and Ran Menika finished her marketing as quickly as she could in order to be with her family before it got dark. It didn't take her more than fifteen minutes to get to her little home but in that short space of time the whole atmosphere of the village seemed to change. In the half light which preceded darkness it was hushed. It was the time when villagers believed that spirits and phantoms begin their nocturnal prowling.

Ran Menika felt a little uneasy that she happened to be returning home so late that day. She recalled the dream of the previous night and a little shudder passed through her body. She wondered for a moment whether it meant bad luck. Was it a warning of things to come? It was in this sombre frame of mind that she turned through the entrance to her home when suddenly a rabbit darted out of the undergrowth, crept swiftly between her feet and disappeared. As the animal brushed past her she felt a sudden charge of fear and a rush of blood through her heart, so much so that she nearly dropped her bag of provisions. She was still trembling when she walked through the gate to her home, trembling so much that the blood seemed to drain out of her face and Juse, who had also returned home, couldn't help but notice the paleness of her features under the rays from the veranda lamp. He reached for the lamp which hung suspended from a beam and turned the flame a little higher, to have a closer look at her. She looked ghastly under the flame.

'What happened?' he asked, trying to conceal his alarm.

'A rabbit . . . a rabbit . . . a . . . a . . .' stuttered Menika finding it difficult to explain what she felt.

'Well. What's wrong about a rabbit?' asked Juse slightly mystified.

'It . . . it . . . darted between my feet and . . . and . . . disappeared,' said Menika still feeling her body tremble with a fear that she couldn't explain.

'Where did it happen?' asked Juse quietly.

'At the gate, just when I was walking through it.'

'But surely, you don't have to fear a rabbit that darts between your feet?'

'I know. I know. But, but, I was still very frightened,' said Menika, her words trailing to a whisper. 'I don't know, I don't know why I should have been so frightened.'

'Come Sudha' (darling), said Juse, slowly, as he relieved his wife of the provisions. 'Let's go to the kitchen and have our meal.'

He sensed at that moment that what his wife needed was solace and a chance to forget, not questions.

Before he went to bed that night Juse was a little perturbed and he could read the look of worry on his wife's face, although she didn't say anything. She seemed to carry out her duties of seeing that the children ate their rice and curry early, in a listless, half hearted manner. She hardly said a word as she gave him, too, his meal and stood by him till he finished. Finally, she ate herself, following the custom, by which she had her meal only after the rest of the household had eaten.

The unusual silence on the part of Ran Menika seemed to depress even the spirits of the children who hardly said a word between them as they ate. On any other occasion there'd generally be a babble of sound from the rickety table at which they sat opposite their father, mildly disputing with each other over something or other.

Juse felt the onset of a sudden uneasiness because of the unaccustomed silence. He was used to laughter and chatter from the children and the bright cheerful voice of his wife who had always something to tell him at dinner time about the village gossip or the antics of the children.

He tried to appear nonchalant. So rising from his seat he closed a window and then switched on the little transistor set which lay on another table. As the cheerful Sinhala music of Sarala Gee (light songs) filled the room with its rhythms, the oppressive atmosphere seemed to lift.

But the music of the radio brought only temporary relief. At eleven o'clock the announcer closed the station for the night and the children had long since gone to sleep on their mats. The silence was disturbing. Apart from a 'Yes' or 'No' Ran Menika had hardly spoken a word. When she got to bed with her husband she moved close to him as if she needed all the protection he could give her.

It didn't take her long to fall asleep but for Juse, to whom sleep usually came quickly, it was different for once. He was worried about his wife's behaviour over the last two days. First she had a terrible dream about his death and then she allowed herself to become scared out of her wits by a rabbit. Try as he might he couldn't fall asleep.

He heard the wall clock in the room strike twelve midnight and with some pride realized that he was one of the few people in the village who could afford such a luxury. The heat in the room was almost unbearable. Not a breath of air stirred, though the window was open. At about half past one Juse found his lids getting heavier and then finally he dozed off.

Suddenly, though, he was jolted awake by a fearsome scream. It was his wife. She had leapt out of the bed and was staring at her husband with a look of terror.

'The doll, the doll,' she shouted wildly. 'It came into my body. It came into my body.'

Those were the last sensible words that Juse heard from

her. Even as he watched her, all his senses alert, yet too shocked to do anything, she began to dance, oblivious of the fact that the cloth she wore around her body was falling to her feet.

It was the wild meaningless dance of a half naked woman who was and yet wasn't his wife. In the light of the moon which filtered through the open window she seemed like a marionette motivated by something other than her own self. She seemed in short, possessed.

For a few moments Juse was just rooted to his bed, watching the weird dance by his wife. No, a thing like this just couldn't happen to his Ran Menika of all people, who hadn't harmed a soul in all her life. But it was happening before his eyes in his very own bedroom. There was no mistaking her stupid, inane, disjointed movements, a hideous parody of a dance. He had seen something similar before when a relative of his had seemingly become possessed by a demon.

Something told Juse that the only remedy was a terrific shock to her system. So raising his hand he slapped her violently across her face. She ceased dancing, gazed at him with just an inkling of recognition and then realizing she was almost naked she bent down, retrieved her cloth and wrapped it round her body. Juse took hold of her hand and gently drew her to the bed. There was a vacant look in her eyes as she gazed towards the window and tears began to trickle down her cheeks. But she was once again, despite the vacant look, more or less, herself.

'What happened to you, Menika?' asked Juse gently as the trembling of her body ceased.

'I had a bad dream.'

'Again?'

'Yes . . .'

'What did you dream?'

But Menika was silent as though reluctant to recall her experience.

'What did you dream?' asked Juse again.

Menika spoke at last with difficulty. 'I dreamt that I was walking alone through our village. In the distance . . . I saw, I saw a cloth doll. It was made of cloth but yet, but yet, it was alive, and it was hideous to look at. It came walking fast, fast, right towards me and then it entered into my body and I screamed. I don't know what happened after that.'

Juse was silent for a few moments, as though collecting his thoughts. Finally he said very quietly, 'Don't you know that you danced before me just a few minutes ago, half naked?'

'No,' said Ran Menika, listlessly. 'I don't know.'

From that moment Juse wondered whether he would have to consult a Kattadiya or sorcerer, one of those who had mastered the art of exorcism, apart from many other accomplishments such as producing charms and talismans. But before he made a final decision he decided to wait another day and see whether the phenomenon happened again.

Juse's worst fears were to be confirmed and, unfortunately, the children were witnesses on the second occasion when their mother rose from her bed possessed by a demon power and began her strange and tortured performance. Very soon everybody in the village knew of what was taking place in the house of Juse. Many were secretly glad and hoped that it would not be easy to find a cure for the stricken woman. Prema and Marthelis, in particular, gloated over the fact that Ran Menika was ill.

'I hope she dances for the rest of her life,' said Prema to her husband when she received the good news.

Marthelis chuckled. 'Our Juse will have to spend a lot of money if he wants to cure his Menika,' he said, 'there are not many Kattadiyas as good as Malhamy.'

Prema agreed. 'I think we had better go tomorrow and pay him,' she said.

Marthelis didn't reply immediately. Money was

always a problem. 'Do you think we can afford the thirty rupees?' he said at last.

'Don't worry,' said Prema. 'I've sold my old pair of earrings.'

Marthelis was shocked. 'What!' he exclaimed. 'Your only pair of earrings?'

'Yes,' said Prema. 'It was worth the sacrifice.'

As Marthelis looked at the large bony features of his wife's face, embittered and hardened by suffering, he knew better than to argue the point.

Meanwhile Juse Appuhamy acted quickly. He journeyed by bus to a village about sixty miles away from his own where he knew of a famous sorcerer called Siyadoris who was said to be even better than Malhamy, though not quite so affluent.

Now Siyadoris, unlike Malhamy, was a thin, fair complexioned man with sunken cheeks and deep set thoughtful eyes. He was well known as a sorcerer who never used his knowledge of the occult to do evil. He lived in a humble little mud hut with a cadjan roof, bordering the main road, and the only other occupant was a youth about twenty-three years in age, who he called his Golea (pupil). This Golea assisted him in all his exorcism ceremonies. When Siyadoris heard Juse's story he was deeply concerned.

'Your wife does seem possessed by a demon,' he said, as he squatted on his veranda, listening to the details. 'But first let us chew on the beetle leaf. It will help us to think clearly.'

Juse accepted the beetle leaf that he was offered and Siyadoris continued. 'I can come to your house in about three days time,' he said, 'but meanwhile I want you to set up two altars made of tender coconut palms. In one of them you must put, on the night of the ceremony, offerings of rice and fruit and flowers. This will be the offering to the Deviyos (deities) who will help me in my efforts to drive the demon out. On the other altar you must have the offerings to the demon, that is, rice, cakes, and meat. Also buy a cock-bird for the occasion just in case the demon expects a live offering.'

When Juse returned home that day he felt much easier in his mind. He had done all he could think of and it now remained for Siyadoris to drive out the demon who had brought misfortune on Menika. On the night of the ceremony, well illuminated by a petromax lamp, Ran Menika was laid on a mat in the garden, her head resting on a pillow, while Siyadoris commenced the overture to the ceremony.

Clad in a simple white banyan and a white sarong with a cylindrical drum slung from his shoulders, he walked up to the altar dedicated to the benevolent spirits or deities, joined his palms together and intoned with bowed head, 'May the blessings of the Deviyos (deities) attend this ceremony. May the demons be driven from the body of this sick woman.'

With these opening words he intoned a few more verses in praise to the benevolent deities and then only began the ceremony proper. Returning to the centre of the clearing in which Ran Menika lay he beat the first clear rhythm on his drum. The rhythm was taken up on a much smaller drum by a local assistant whom he had hired for the occasion. Thus bass and treble drums combined to produce the first weird rhythms of the Yak Natum (Devil Dance).

As the weird, yet deeply melodious, throb of the drums was heard, someone burst through the crowd of villagers who had gathered to watch the ceremony, and with a great leap commenced to dance. This was the sorcerer's Golea or pupil who wore on his head a hideous wooden mask. Huge black eye-balls jutted out of the mask, painted garishly in red. From a gaping cavern of a mouth flanked by fierce looking tusks, white teeth projected. The nose was curved like the beak of a hawk.

Above the head of the mask slender cobras, beautifully carved, wound their way upwards till their puffed hoods met in the centre. A white banyan, flouncing red skirt and white stockings from thighs to ankles completed the ensemble of the dancer.

Ran Menika meanwhile, lay on the mat, a sheet covering her up to the shoulders. Her lips seemed bloodless in the bluish light from the lamp and damp wisps of hair straggled over her face. Her eyes had sunk deep in their sockets and were gazing blankly at the dancer. A few solicitous relatives sat by her side fanning her with folded newspapers. These were the women, who, fortunately for Juse, had taken things over when they realized that Ran Menika was in no condition to attend to her daily work.

The dancer continued leaping to the rhythm of the drums. In one hand he held a glowing faggot which he waved about his body creating intricate lines of light as he danced. At intervals he threw some inflammable powder on the torch and great tongues of flame leapt skywards, flushing the darkness of the trees for an instant with amber.

At about two o'clock in the morning Ran Menika, who hitherto had been on her mat, gazing fixedly at the dancer, as though mesmerized by his movements, suddenly came alive. She leapt up from her mat, flung the sheet that covered her, aside, and stared with bloodshot eyes at the dancer.

Siyadoris, who as master of ceremonies had been watching everything, increased the tempo of his rhythm. Faster and faster he beat the drum until the tempo became a frenzy. The dancer became a whirling mass of movement, so fast that one could barely distinguish the outlines of his body.

Ran Menika, meanwhile began to tremble. She looked terror stricken at the crowd around her and tried to escape but immediately her relatives held her arms.

Suddenly her body heaved. She struggled violently before collapsing in a swoon.

The dancer, too, at this moment was galvanized into a final burst of movement which he kept up for almost ten minutes. Then spent he too heeled over. While he was still on the floor in his hideous mask, Siyadoris advanced towards him.

'Who are you?' he asked the fallen dancer in a tone of authority.

'I am Kalu Kumara,' said the dancer, in a voice which seemed peculiarly high-pitched.

'Kalu Kumara, the Black Prince, himself.'

The onlookers gasped as they heard the reply. Kalu Kumara, they knew, was a demon of great power who generally tormented women. But Siyadoris was by no means awed. He was truly master of the situation.

'Have you left the woman?'

'Yes,' said the high pitched voice, 'but only for a moment.'

'And now you possess the body of my golea?'

'Yes.'

'Leave him, too. Leave the vicinity of the woman for good.'

'No. I will not leave.'

'Leave him immediately,' shouted Siyadoris.

'No, no,' said the voice, its high-pitched tone becoming almost a shriek. 'I will not leave till you have given me an offering.'

'What offering do you want? We have laid out rice, cakes and flesh for you on your altar. What more do you want?

'I want a live offering.'

'Will a cock-bird suffice?'

For a moment there was silence, as dancer and sorcerer gazed at each other, one on the ground and the other standing menacingly above him. Finally the high-pitched voice said, 'A young cock-bird will suffice.'

'If we offer you a cock-bird,' said the sorcerer, 'what sign will you give us that you've left the vicinity of the woman for good.'

'I will tear a branch off the Jak Tree in this garden.'

The sorcerer gave a sign to Juse who had bought a young cock-bird for this eventuality. The bird was given to the dancer who with both hands held it aloft by the neck. The crowd surged closer. There was a moment of silence and then a collective gasp of horror as the dancer tore the bird's neck apart with his powerful hands, and dropped it on the ground. Someone picked up the bouncing cock-bird with the severed spinal column and took it to the altar of the demon.

A few minutes later there was an ear splitting sound and a huge branch of a Jak Tree in the garden crashed down to earth. The villagers scurried to avoid it. Meanwhile, the dancer too had fallen into a swoon and lay limply, limbs stretched out on the sand. The sorcerer sprinkled some water on his face and body and recovering, he rose slowly and pulled off the mask that he wore.

Ran Menika, too, had risen from her mat and from that moment onwards she began talking to Juse Appuhamy and all those who surrounded her as though nothing had happened. Among the many onlookers there were two people who were bitterly disappointed and furious at the successful outcome of the ceremony – Prema and her husband Marthelis.

Neither Juse nor his wife suspected the evil role that their neighbours had played in this grim affair. But when a week later Prema was found dead on her mat one morning by her husband, with a look of terror in her staring eyes, they began to wonder. It is a common belief in villages that when a person harnesses the aid of a demon, he or she runs the risk of death at the hands of this same demon, should their sinister purpose fail.

White Lady of the Hohenzollerns

Clyde Clarke

The Royal Palace in Berlin was ablaze with light. Before the dressing-table in her boudoir the Queen smiled at her reflection in the mirror. She was wearing a gown of ivory brocade embroidered in silver that she had secretly ordered from her native Hanover. Opening a silver-bound casket, she lifted glittering jewels and let them slip through her fingers, joyously, as a child might play with running water. To her they represented buried hopes and vanished dreams, and tonight she was to wear them again after many years. There was the diadem she had worn as the bride of Frederick William I, the diamond necklace her brother had sent at the birth of her first child, and the bracelet her husband had clasped upon her arm when at last, after fervent prayers and long waiting, their son, the future Frederick the Great, was born.

She rose and surveyed herself in the long Venetian mirror and was almost happy. Then Princess Ulrica came in.

'Gracious, mama,' she exclaimed, 'you look as if

Heaven and all its stars had fallen upon you. You are beautiful! Did our most Royal King and father command you to appear tonight in those lovely jewels?'

'Hush, child! You know how the King despises ornaments and luxuries. If he could see me he would die with rage.'

'No, sweet mamma, he would calculate how many giant soldiers he could hire for his personal Guard for the price of this necklace, or how many miles of military roads he could build with this diadem.'

'Don't speak of the King, child! Think of other things, of whom you will command to dance with you at the ball this evening. Your father will soon be thinking of a prince for you, for he intends you to be a Queen.'

'I will marry whom I please,' the little Princess said haughtily, 'and I shall wear diamonds every day if I wish to. I will not be miserable as poor brother Frederick is.'

'If your father commands, you must obey – as we all do,' Sophia sighed, kissing her daughter lightly on the cheek.

They went into the ante-room, and at that moment Poellnitz, the Grand Chamberlain at the Court of King Frederick the First, threw open the doors and announced that the guests were assembled.

As they followed the Grand Chamberlain through the crowd of richly dressed women and men covered with stars and orders, Sophia managed to whisper to Ulrica: 'The King has commanded us to be merry tonight. And take care, child, Frederick has spies everywhere. When you speak to Poellnitz, remember that he repeats every word to the King.'

After making the grand tour of the *salons* the Queen seated herself at a card-table with the Margrafin Maria Dorothea and the English and French Ambassadors. Never had she been more gracious, more queenly. Behind her chair stood two maids of honour. She turned to them now and then to give some order or to send them to look after the young princesses, who were dancing in the next *salon*.

Suddenly the music ceased. The May evening seemed very still. An ominous silence oppressed the room. Then, from the other wing of the palace came the sound of loud knocking – hammer blows resounding in slow, solemn rhythm.

The Duke of Holstein spoke to General Schwerin, so that the Queen might hear: 'Is the King at work in his carpentry shop? I thought he could not leave his chair.'

'They say he has worked all day at his carpentering,' the General replied. 'He thinks his gout will be better and his arms and legs will be less stiff if he uses them.'

The Queen tried to smile and go on with the game. She turned to Poellnitz who was standing near: 'Why does the music stop? Do have them play on. It is so much more cheerful.'

She played her cards absently, as the music started again. Then she turned to one of her maids of honour: 'Have the princesses come to me as soon as the dance is over,' she commanded, her face grave.

But before the command could be obeyed, the Princess Amelia, pale and horrified, rushed to her mother, greatly agitated.

'My dear child, what is wrong?' the Queen cried.

'The Lady in White!' Amelia whispered, her voice trembling. 'I saw her as I looked out the window. She was moving among the lilac bushes!'

The Queen turned pale. She rose instantly and in another moment all were standing. In the tomb-like stillness that fell over the rooms they could hear the rhythmic beat of the hammer in the other wing of the palace. A faint perfume of lilacs was in the air.

The Grand Chamberlain came very softly to the Queen's side. He bowed. 'Your Majesty, command me!' he said, his voice a trifle unsteady.

'Has anyone else seen "The Lady in White"?' she asked, anxiously.

'Yes, Your Majesty. Several of the sentries have seen the spectre, but not in this part of the palace. The figure was seen floating – '

'Where?' she whispered. 'Floating where? Tell me.'

'In the gardens and around the corridors of the other wing of the palace.'

The Queen recovered herself quickly: 'I command that the dance proceed!' She was still very pale, but she turned to soothe Princess Amelia. 'It is nothing, child, it is but a myth. Go back to your dancing and be gay. Remember, we are commanded by the King to be happy tonight.'

Amelia went away reluctantly with a young margrave who had accompanied her, and the Queen talked in whispers to General Schwerin.

The English Ambassador was curious, and he asked the French Ambassador, in a low voice: 'The Lady in White? Who is she? I do not understand.'

'It is the legendary spectre that has haunted the ruling family of Prussia for centuries,' the French Ambassador whispered. 'It always portends the death of a member of the Imperial family. If it wears white gloves, it means a woman is to die; if black gloves, it means the death of a man. It is said always to appear before the death of a Royal personage.'

As the music started again the Queen resumed her seat at the card-table and calmly arranged her cards. 'Let us play,' she said.

In the wing of the palace occupied by the King, there was silence. Frederick William sat alone in his bare room. Slowly he raised himself from his chair and extended his arms.

'They think I am suffering, chained to my chair!' he cried. 'But I have no pain tonight. The work has cured the pain!' He stretched his arms and moved his fingers gleefully.

'They think that the doors of the Royal vault will soon open to receive my corpse. But Frederick William will not die! My son shall not reign! This weak, riotous youth, this dreamer! Prussia has no need of this sentimental boy, who finds the tones of his flute sweeter than the sounds of trumpets and drums! Never shall Prussia be ruled by a dreaming poet!'

His breath came fast. He was trembling with rage. 'Bah! the fool has said that Voltaire was as great as a king – yes, greater than the kings anointed by the Pope! A fool shall not govern Prussia. The King will live!'

Worn out by this outburst, he sank into his chair again, murmuring: 'They think I shall die, but I shall be well. I have commanded Sophia to give a ball that the world could see that the Queen and my daughters are gay and happy!'

He called the servant who awaited his pleasure in the adjoining room and commanded him: 'Call together the gentlemen who compose my Tobacco Club, and arrange everything for a meeting of that august body!'

'But those gentlemen, Your Majesty, are at the Queen's ball,' the servant said, astonished.

'Then go for them. Bring them quickly. Poellnitz must come, and Eckert, and Baron von Goltz and Hacke, Duke of Holstein, and General Schwerin. Quick! In ten minutes they must all be here, but,' he cautioned, raising a shaking finger, 'let no one know why he is sent for. Only whisper to each one that he is commanded to come to me. Tell him he must tell no one where he is going. I will not have the Queen's ball disturbed. She must be happy tonight! Go!'

In ten minutes six gentlemen, their faces very pale, stood in the King's ante-chamber.

'What does this sudden summons mean?' they asked each other anxiously. No one knew.

The servant entered the King's room. His Majesty, dressed in the full uniform of his Guard, sat at a round table, on which the pipes and the mugs filled with foaming beer were already placed. He had condescended to fill a pipe with his own hands, and was on the point of lighting it at a nearby candle.

'Sire,' the servant said, 'the gentlemen are waiting in the ante-room.'

'Do they know why I have sent for them?' the King asked, blowing a cloud of smoke from his mouth.

'Your Majesty forbade me to tell them.'

'Well, go now and tell them I am more furiously angry today than you have ever seen me, that I am standing by the door with my crutch, and that I command them to come singly into my presence.'

'What is the matter? Why is the King so angry? What orders do you bring from His Majesty?' the men questioned the servant in anxious whispers.

The servant assumed a terrified expression as he replied: 'His Majesty has never been so outrageously angry. Woe unto him over whom the cloud bursts. He commands that each you enter the room alone. Go now! For heaven's sake do not keep the King waiting. I fear for what may happen to you!'

The men looked at each other in consternation. No one wished to be first to encounter the King's rage.

The Grand Chamberlain, bowing to the Duke of Holstein, said: 'Your Grace has precedence.'

The Duke winced. 'No,' he said, 'you are well aware that His Majesty does not regard Court etiquette on these occasions, and would be most indignant if we paid any attention to it. Let us not displease him. Go first yourself, my dear friend.'

'Not I, Your Grace. I would not dare to take precedence in this group. The King would be angry with me. If you decline the honour, it is due to General Schwerin.'

'Gentlemen,' interrupted the servant, 'His Majesty will become impatient and then more angry.'

'But, my God, who will dare go first?' Count von Goltz cried.

'I will,' said Councillor Eckert. 'I owe everything to His Majesty, I will place my life at his service.' He braced himself, and with firm steps went to the door and opened it.

His companions saw the King's eyes flash as he raised his crutch over the head of his favourite, and then the door closed. Though they heard no sound, they waited anxiously.

Poellnitz spoke to the servant in faltering tones: 'Against which of us is the anger of the King directed? Is it I?'

'Alas, I do not know,' the servant replied. 'Let the next one enter. His Majesty must not be kept waiting.'

Poellnitz stepped boldly to the door, and as he entered they saw the King standing in threatening attitude inside the door. Each time this scene was repeated, and then General Schwerin, the last of the six, went in to the King's presence.

This time the King was not standing at the door. He lay in his arm-chair, laughing until the tears rolled down his withered cheeks.

'The joke succeeded to perfection,' he said, exultantly. 'Even you, Schwerin, who never knew fear on the battlefield, are trembling with fear.'

The General tried to smile: 'Yes, Sire, a shot is a trifling thing compared with a flash from your eyes. I have no fear of death, I only fear the displeasure of my sovereign.'

'Give me your hand, Schwerin,' the old monarch said. 'You are a brave fellow. And now, gentlemen, away with all constraint and etiquette. We will suppose the King to be at the ball. I am only your companion, Frederick William. I will now proceed to the opening of the

Tobacco Club. Tell your very best guardroom jokes. Make me laugh!'

The big empty room was lighted by but four tallow candles, for the King would tolerate nothing beyond bare necessities, and the four streaks of light seemed pale and sickly in the blue smoke that filled the air.

'Light more candles,' the King commanded his man-in-waiting. 'Our Tobacco Club must present a festive appearance tonight so that the contrast between it and the ball be not too great.' Then he spoke to the Grand Chamberlain: 'Tell me, Poellnitz, is the Queen's ball a brilliant one? The Queen – is she gay, and are the princesses dancing merrily?'

'I have never witnessed a more magnificent spectacle, Sire, nor has Her Majesty ever been more beautiful. I had no idea she possessed such priceless jewels.'

The King's face set in its accustomed hard lines. 'Fill the glasses, Jochen,' he said to the valet. Then a harsh laugh escaped his lips. 'So she has put on her jewels, has she? They are taking advantage of my absence. They think I am writhing on a bed of pain.'

Poellnitz put down his mug and smiled. 'The Queen has good reason for being happy tonight, for Your Majesty is not ill. You have worked all day in your carpentering shop. In the ballroom above the music we could hear the blows of your hammer.'

Frederick took a long draught of beer, and the lid snapped loudly as he banged the mug on the table. 'I should not be surprised if Frederick had clandestinely come over to this ball,' he said. 'He thinks to govern Prussia with his book-learning and his poems. A dreaming scholar can never be a good king. He who wields pen and fiddle-bow instead of a sword and sceptre, will never be a good general.'

Poellnitz set down his mug quietly and said quickly, in soothing tones: 'Your Majesty forgets that this is a sitting of the Tobacco Club and not of the State Council. Let us be gay as the others are gay tonight. Your pipe is out and your mug is empty, Sire!'

'True,' said Frederick. 'Fill my mug, Jochen, I shall drink to the health of him who first overcame fear and dared to enter this room. Who was it? I have forgotten. You are all cowards in my presence. Raise your glasses! Drink!'

'The toast is to the Privy Councillor von Eckert, Sire,' said Count Hacke with an ironical smile.

'He entered the chamber as he goes into battle,' Poellnitz laughed, 'in the spirit in which he took leave of all the fine breweries and artfully constructed non-smoke chimneys which he built. He marched courageously into the Royal presence.' The King's favourite was far from popular with the other officers.

Eckert's face was pale in the flickering light, and he scowled at Poellnitz, as the other men laughed heartily.

'Really, your wit this evening is dazzling, Poellnitz,' he said. 'I am charmed with your pleasantries.'

'Silence!' Frederick commanded. 'No more of this raillery.'

Suddenly the door opened and the King's valet appeared.

'Your Majesty,' he said, 'your orders have been obeyed. The White Salon is ready. The last work of your hands has been placed there for your inspection. The paint is quite dry.'

'Illumine the White Salon!' Frederick cried, struggling to his feet and throwing his mug on the table. 'Jochen, give me your arm!'

In the grand ball-room the music went on without pause at the Queen's demand. The May air was soft and the scent of lilacs drifted through the open windows. The face of the Queen was pale but very sweet under the glittering diadem, and she tried to smile as she played her cards.

Suddenly the Princess Sophia Dorothea, who stood nearby, gave a low cry of terror and fell back into the arms of a maid of honour. 'The King!' she whispered. 'My God, the King!'

In the corridor, approaching the doorway, they saw Frederick, his eyes flashing, his limbs trembling. Supported by his valets, he came slowly towards the room.

The Queen whispered to the attendant behind her: 'Remove my long ear-rings and the necklace quickly!' Then she calmly played a queen on the table before her. The French Ambassador played a king.

'Lost!' she said, trying to smile. 'So must the Queen ever be lost when the King comes.'

Frederick fixed his blazing eyes upon her and called her name. A hush fell over the room. She rose instantly and went to him, a faint smile on her pale face.

'Ah, my husband,' she said, 'what a pleasant surprise you have prepared for us! It is most amiable of Your Majesty to honour this feast with your presence.'

The King grasped her arm savagely and his voice was harsh: 'It is necessary in the midst of earthly pleasures to be reminded of the fleeting vanity of earthly things. I am come to administer this medicine to your vain and sin-sick soul. Come with me! All of you. Follow me! Let none remain behind!'

In vain the Queen pleaded with Frederick to tell her his plan. She could only walk tremblingly at his side and go with him. She knew not where.

The King kept his eyes steadily before him. His face was set and hard. He did not speak. The bejewelled ladies and gentlemen of his Court followed the Royal pair in a long, glittering procession. No one dared to disobey the King's orders. Though it looked like a wedding procession, the courtiers and their ladies felt as if they were marching towards their doom.

The Queen looked anxiously from side to side, anticipating some new terror as the long parade passed through the flower-decked dressing-rooms, through the brilliantly lighted ante-chamber, on through the endless corridors and up the long staircase, until at last they reached the door of the White Salon, which Frederick had built and adorned.

At the King's command the doors were thrown open and he led Sophia into the room.

She gave a cry of horror: *'Two coffins! Your Majesty – what does this mean?'*

'Yes, two coffins, mine and yours. I have made them with my own hands. I finished them tonight – while you revelled. In these coffins we will soon rest and all earthly vanity and glory will be at an end. No one will then fear my glances or my crutch. No one will admire the glittering jewels of the Queen. Dust will return to dust and the King and Queen will be nothing more than food for worms.'

Under the crystal chandeliers the lights glared in the marble whiteness of the room. For a moment no one moved or breathed.

Then Sophia summoned her courage and spoke softly: 'Not so, my King! The dust of common mortals will be scattered in every direction by the hand of Time. But from our dust history will build enduring monuments!'

As she spoke the Queen seemed endowed with fresh beauty. She needed no royal diadem, no gleaming jewels to enhance her queenly bearing. She was the wife of the King of Prussia, the sister of the King of England, the mother of the future King of the Prussian Empire.

Her composure angered Frederick. With a trembling hand he pointed to the statues of his ancestors that adorned the room. His tone was imperious, terrifying: 'So, then, let my ancestors see how well we will look in our coffins! The world knows that jewels become you and that I am a fine fellow in my uniform, but let us try our coffins!'

The Queen faltered: 'Oh, my King – '

'Do not waste precious time – you have wasted enough at the card-table this evening. See if you can take your place with grace and dignity in this coffin I have made for you with my own hands. Lay yourself in your coffin, Sophia, that I may see a picture of you that you can never behold. I have brought you here that we may try our coffins.'

'This is a cruel jest, Frederick!' There was a tremor in her voice, but she turned to one of her maids of honour and said: 'Duchess, give me your hand. I am very weary, and for a time I shall rest in peace upon this bed.'

As the Duchess took her trembling hand, the Queen lifted the skirt of her royal robe slightly and stepped over the edge of the coffin. Proudly erect she stood for a moment and then, with dainty grace, she stooped and stretched her body until with closed eyes she lay still and calm in the white coffin.

The rudely made coffin creaked and groaned. A murmur of horror came from the richly attired company.

The King stood looking on, his features set in cruel lines. After a few moments Sophia opened her eyes and looked up at him. His eyes avoided hers and he stared at the floor.

Slowly the Queen arose, very pale, but with her imperial dignity unbent. The Duchess held out a hand to assist her, but she declined it saying: 'Kings and queens must leave their coffins by their own strength and greatness, sustained by their deeds alone.'

With these words she stepped over the edge of the coffin and bowing profoundly to the King, said: 'Your Majesty, it is your turn now.'

The King looked at her darkly and stepped awkwardly into his coffin. He called some of his courtiers to assist him in lying down. 'Here I will soon sleep,' he said.

Sophia reached her hand to him. 'May that time be far removed, my King,' she said.

At that moment the awed silence of the room was

broken by loud piercing cries and the sound of hastening feet in the ante-chamber.

Frederick sat bolt upright in his coffin, a look of terror in his drawn face: 'What is it? What has happened? I demand to know!'

The major-domo stepped forward with shaking limbs: 'Your Majesty, the sentries in the corridor have seen the figure of a tall woman clad in white – she passed the whole length of the corridor and entered this room!'

'The Lady in White!' cried Frederick, falling as if broken to pieces in his coffin. The courtiers recoiled and the ladies stood paralyzed with amazed horror. Only the Queen was calm.

Frederick suddenly sat up in his coffin and asked in a creaking voice: 'Did she wear white gloves or black?'

For a moment no one spoke. A deep silence pervaded the room. The scent of lilacs drifted in from the palace gardens.

At last the major-domo dared to break the silence: 'She wore black gloves, Your Majesty.'

'Black! That means I am to die,' Frederick cried. 'Help me from this coffin! You will put me back soon enough!'

As morning dawned, Her Majesty, the Queen, stood at the window of her apartment and looked out into the mist of the new May day. White lilacs hung in pallid clusters from bending boughs. Birds twittered softly among the leaves. Ghostly swans swam placidly, skirting the water-lilies on the border of the lake.

Beyond all that she could see with her eyes was the castle at Rheinsberg, where the Prince Royal was sleeping peacefully, his flute on the table at his bedside.

In his bare room across the misty garden the King lay dying. She knew that the time was at hand when Frederick William II, afterwards known as Frederick the Great, was to ascend the throne of Prussia.